827

D0364682

GAMMON AND ESPIONAGE

GAMMON
AND ESPIONAGE

★

NICOLAS BENTLEY

who also drew the pictures

THE CRESSET PRESS LTD.
11 FITZROY SQUARE,
LONDON, W.1

First published 1938

827 ✓

Made *and* printed *in* Great Britain
By The Camelot Press Ltd
London *and* Southampton

DEDICATED

to the memory of "Sapper" for
Bull-Dog Drummond,

to that of Edgar Wallace for
The Squeaker,

to W. Somerset Maugham for
Ashenden,

to Valentine Williams for
The Man with the Clubfoot,

to John Buchan for
The Thirty-Nine Steps,

to E. Phillips Oppenheim for
The Spy Paramount,

to Sax Rohmer for
Dr. Fu Manchu,

and to Sydney Horler for
the fun of the thing.

CONTENTS

7

LIST OF ILLUSTRATIONS

CHAPTER I

THE GIRL IN THE CARLTON BAR

THERE were four of us in this affair, and we were thrown together as a palsied man might throw a pair of dice. Though we hardly knew each other we all became friends from the start, and like a dental student with his first patient, we sustained ourselves by mutual sympathy throughout the whole nerve-racking adventure.

I suppose it is part of the natural contrariness of life that I, with my philosophic instincts, should so often have been chosen rather than, say, Sir Archibald Sinclair, as the blunt instrument of Fate. Life for a great many people turns out to be monotonous beyond the expectations of a goldfish, but I cannot complain that I have not had a fairly generous slice of its excitements.

These began soon after Oxford got me down, when I went into the diplomatic service and was sent out as a special emissary among the Kurds. Later I swopped their nomadic hospitality for the ranks of the Papal Guard. And once, for a short while, I was a courier of the Tsar, and then of the *Huddersfield Gazette*.

But when my part in this peculiar story began

I was again attached to the Foreign Office, though only by the frailest regard for duty. Times were rather troubled, and as usual the air was full of rumours. The situation was one that needed to be handled with a good deal of prudence, but all the same, when the flat season came to an end I had still not picked a single winner. I had never known such a state of affairs to happen before. In fact, for a long period my luck had been exceptional. But now, from time to time, a spectral image of the Official Receiver began to rise up and dance a melancholy *pavane* across the background of my dreams.

One evening as I walked home from Whitehall I was turning the whole situation over in my mind. And presently, in the oblivion of my thoughts, as you may often see a familiar face or gesture without recognising it, I found that I was floating through the passages of the Carlton Hotel.

Then, still floating, I came into the Bar. There were not more than a few people there, but in one corner I noticed a girl sitting alone. Though she had on a veil I could see that the face underneath it was a beautiful one. She was dressed quietly but extremely well; her only sign of jewellery was a large *cabochon* emerald, which glittered from a disappointingly flat bosom.

Facing her across the room there was an

odd-looking man of about fifty, from whose appearance, and the fact that he was reading *Die Geflügel Welt*, I took to be a foreigner. On his head was a large muff made of grey astrakhan.

Much to my surprise the girl spoke to me in a low voice as I passed her:

"Waiter," she said, "I'll have the same again."

I hesitated for a second or two, not knowing quite how to accept the situation. To refuse the order, I thought, would show her the mistake she had made, and if the privilege of embarrassing her was to be mine I would rather have chosen my own time and place. So I nodded quickly to her, and then went across to the bar. As I sat up on one of the high stools I gave her order to the barman; then I looked along the diverting array of bottles in front of me for some inspiration. A glass of sherry, I thought, would be an excellent thing, but being distrustful of first impressions I ordered a large brandy and soda instead.

I was thinking, as I began to drink, that there was something in the girl's voice that had seemed familiar to me, and as I looked towards her I tried to recall where we might possibly have met. Presently, when she lifted her veil to blow the froth from her glass, I saw her face. It was a face which, seeing it suddenly like that, could

not have startled me more if it had been A. P.
Herbert's. But it was not; it was that of Captain
Poodle Grummond, or as I knew him to be,
H_2O of His Majesty's Intelligence Service.

I was never more surprised in my life, and after
the first shock of seeing him in this disguise,
which I imagined was the reason for his wearing
the Lanvin model he had got on, I slipped from
my stool. A waiter helped me to my feet, and I
went quickly across the room. Poodle saw me as I
came over to him, and he drew down his veil.
But when I greeted him he gave me his hand
and said in very shrill tones:

"My dear!" *How* nice it is to see you!"

His expression struck me as being rather bored
and supercilious, and the inconsistency of this
with his gushing manner gave me the exact
impression of a witless society woman. I took
the lead which he offered and tried to fall in
cautiously with what was going on. But for me it
was like playing a game without any idea of the
rules or the stakes. He talked for some time about
people and events that I knew nothing of, and to
avoid floundering I hardly said more than a few
words. But Poodle seemed to know the latest
scandal about every *Tatler* beauty, and I was on
the point of dozing off when he changed his tone.
It dropped an octave or two and he said quietly:

"What brought you here?"

I told him, and then we began to talk about old times. It was a little over two years since we had seen each other, and looking at him now as an experienced and attractive woman it was difficult to remember that when we had last met he had suddenly appeared as a postman in Bettws-y-Coed. He was then on some sort of secret mission, of course, but I had never been more surprised in my life.

Sometimes I felt that I rather envied him his job with all its excitement and its variety of strange experiences. But in comparison with the inconvenience and danger of it the returns seemed pretty poor, though there were compensations, of course, for anyone who enjoyed a perpetual change of scenery and sex.

It was naturally difficult for me to hide my curiosity about his latest adventures, which I knew had been strange and numerous, but I was even more inquisitive to know the explanation of his present incognito.

After we had been talking for a little while he nodded towards the man with the muff on his head, who was now reading *Die Meerschweinchen Woche*.

"Ever heard of Doctor Rudolf Schmutzig?" he said.

"Heard of him? I said: "of course."

"That's him."

I was never more surprised in my life, though Poodle had showed him to me with apparently as little expectation of my interest as if he were pointing out Godfrey Winn to Professor Gilbert Murray.

But his words needed no under-emphasis to give them reality. Looking at the face under the astrakhan muff, at that resolute expression, at those hard eyes and faintly smiling lips, you could imagine easily enough that this was a man whom the great powers looked upon not merely as a bold and unscrupulous spy but as a perfect nuisance.

Poodle took out a small *Fabergé* cigarette case from his bag. It was typical, I thought, that even in a temporary change of sex the instinctive elegance and taste which characterised him as a man should have persisted in him as a woman.

He leant forward, and as I held my lighter to his cigarette he whispered to me:

"We can't talk here. You must follow me when I leave. But until one of my men shows up I've got to keep Schmutzig in sight."

A little later on an enormous man appeared in the doorway.

"Ah, that's Midget," Poodle said. "He's the house detective."

Mr. Midget looked about him casually as he came in. His back was towards me for some

Those hard eyes and faintly smiling lips.

moments, and at first I could not be sure whether he had noticed Doctor Schmutzig. Then he winced sharply and turned towards the bar; I knew that he had seen him.

"I'm rather afraid Doctor Rudolf may give us a little trouble," Poodle said. "He's inclined to be inquisitive, and they think at H.Q. that he may have wind——"

"It does look rather like it," I said.

I saw the grey muff shake gently as a silent eructation rocked the spy.

"I mean that he has wind of our new B.O. plan," Poodle said.

I already knew enough about the mysterious missions that Poodle undertook from time to time to feel surprised no longer at the nature of these, however fantastic they might seem. But this one did sound a little out of the ordinary, and what the nature or purpose might be of something that was called a B.O. plan was outside my rather elementary knowledge of tactics and strategy.

Poodle looked round, and when he was satisfied that no one was in hearing he leant over towards me.

"The B.O. plan is the latest and most important factor in the organisation for civilian defence," he said.

"I see. But why is it called B.O.?" I asked.

"God knows!" Poodle said reverently. "As a

matter of fact, I've got it with me now." He tapped his thigh: "It's in my stocking."

Presently, when we had finished our drinks, he said:

"Well, until my man shows up I think we might safely leave Rudolf with the house dick."

He looked towards Mr. Midget who seemed to understand from Poodle's expression what was expected of him. The detective put a finger in one of his nostrils, then he blew out his huge cheeks and rolled his eyes slowly round and round. Poodle answered this cabalistic panto-mime with a slight nod, and then we got up to go.

We walked slowly together up Haymarket. The evening was warm, and long shadows fell compassionately on a gigantic smirking face that hung across the façade of the Carlton Cinema.

"Don't look back," Poodle said presently with an odd smile, "I have a feeling, though, that we're being followed."

We stopped in front of a window, and in a few minutes the plate glass reflected a figure who was watching both of us intently. Between him and ourselves there was a group of shoppers at a bus stop, where they were waiting with that vacuous air of resignation that many people like them will probably wear at the sounding of the Last Trump. Above their heads rose the un-mistakable reflection of Doctor Schmutzig's muff.

Poodle walked quickly to the edge of the pavement and hailed a taxi.

"Holborn Baths!" he said in tones loud enough for the Doctor to overhear.

We swerved into Orange Street, and in a minute or so Poodle pushed back the window and re-directed the driver to Billingsgate. At Ludgate Circus he gave him fresh instructions to go to Kew Gardens via Blackwall Tunnel, and then changed his mind again, so that we were soon heading for Quaglino's instead. In this way we travelled from King's Cross to Queen's Park, passing Tattersall's and Camberwell Polytechnic on the way.

It was fascinating to see Poodle's ingenuity in trying to throw Doctor Schmutzig off our track. But I was not sorry when we drew up in Whitehall after two hours of continuous driving.

As we came to a stop a figure suddenly pitched into the gutter from behind our taxi and a grey astrakhan muff fell on the dusty pavement. We turned and saw Schmutzig snatch up his headgear and hurry away. I was never more surprised in my life, and for a few seconds we simply stared after him in silence.

As he made off towards Trafalgar Square we saw that in his hand he was carrying a dry-fly fishing-rod.

CHAPTER II

SIR HUGO

WE went into the building quickly, and as we walked up the main staircase and along a corridor Poodle stripped off his disguise.

He had reached a point where I was beginning to feel a little embarrassed by the attention which his *déshabillé* attracted from the clerks who passed us, when we stopped in front of a door. By this time, having shed most of his clothes with the ease of a python discarding its skin, he was dressed in very little more than a pink chemise. He knocked on the door and without waiting for an answer we went inside. The room was large and furnished like many other rooms in Whitehall with that leathern cheerlessness so dear to the official mind.

A window faced the door, and in front of it stood a great desk, from which a man got up as he came in. He had a thin, florid face and a grey moustache. His head was bald and pink, and his cheeks and eyes were pink, too; under his eyes there were neat grey bags, and when he moved away from his desk I saw that he wore another pair of these lower down.

As he got up to greet us a typist slipped off his knee. She was fair with the sort of face that Ethel Mannin might call a madonna's, though with this, I think, Correggio would probably not have agreed. Her hair was a little too slick and the colour of her mouth too vivid; but she had eyes that were remarkable, like her knees, for their prettiness.

As she got up she looked with confusion and a certain amount of envy at Poodle's chemise and then went quickly out of the room.

"Bring us some more cups, will you, Miss Plimsoll?" the man with pink eyes said: "and get something for Captain Grummond to put on." He turned to Poodle. "You'd like some tea, I expect?"

"We should be very thankful for some," Poodle said. He then introduced us.

"Sir Hugo Hugo."

The older man bowed and took my hand limply in his own.

"How do you do? How do you do?" I said.

"How do you do?" Sir Hugo said.

"How do *you* do?" said Poodle. Sir Hugo's manner was so vague and expansive that he might as well have been addressing Poodle as myself.

"How do you do?" he repeated to Poodle.

"How do you do?"

22

"How do you do? How do you do?"

They bowed, and then to make quite sure Sir Hugo bowed once more towards me.

"How do you do?"

"How do you do?" I murmured.

"Skip it," Sir Hugo said.

In a few minutes Miss Plimsoll came back with a bath wrap and two more cups. She handed the wrap to Poodle and put the cups down on a tea-tray which stood among the illustrated papers, racing specials and golf clubs on Sir Hugo's desk. There was a particular grace about her movements that you could not help noticing in everything she did. As she went out of the room Sir Hugo looked reflectively towards her.

"Nice pair of legs," he said quietly to no one in particular. Then he turned to me.

"Milk *and* sugar?" he said, pouring out some tea. "Or lemon?" He added this as though it were a caprice to which the hospitality of his department could only extend itself with difficulty.

"Lemon, please," I said.

He looked silently at the tray for some moments.

"There isn't any," he said sadly. "When I was in Russia before the War we always had lemon with everything." He spoke with the air of a man who knows that for him the pleasures of life are over, and that resignation is the true test of a martyr. "I remember Tchehov once coming to our house," he said, "and when my mother asked

24

him what he liked in his tea he said the answer
was a lemon. It must have been his birthday, I
think. Anyway, he was all in black, and I shall
never forget his finger-nails as long as I live."

Sir Hugo sipped at his lemonless tea and there
was silence for a little while. Then Poodle began
to tell him what had happened to us while we
were first of all watching and then trying to rid
ourselves of Doctor Schmutzig.

"But what are these plans that you mention?"
Sir Hugo said.

"You know, the B.O. ones," Poodle said.

"Oh, *those*——"

Again Sir Hugo said nothing for a while, but
sat at the desk tapping his fingers on the inkstand,
which, according to a small gold plate on the
front of it, had seen better days as the foot of an
elephant called Gustave, who had been present
at the Delhi Durbar of 1911. There were still a
few traces of gilt on the huge toe-nails, though
that was all that was left to remind you of this
spectacular happening in what was otherwise
probably rather a monotonous life. *Sic transit
gloria mundi*, I thought, as I read the rather
pathetic little inscription.

"May I have a look at that plan?" Sir Hugo
said presently. He held out his hand across the
desk.

Poodle felt in the top of his silk stocking, and

his face suddenly changed. He looked up quickly.

"Sir Hugo—it's gone," he said.

I was never more surprised in my life. His voice was steady but I knew the tone of it well enough to realise how bitterly he was disappointed by the discovery.

"Gone?" Sir Hugo said.

"Honestly, look——!" Poodle pulled back his dressing-gown to show the top of his stocking and the frills on his chemise.

"Please——" Sir Hugo said in a faint voice. He looked out of the window as he spoke, but I could see for myself that except for Poodle's muscular leg the stocking was quite empty.

"This is very distressing," Sir Hugo said. "Do you know that I had nearly completed a chess problem on the margin of that plan? Well, we must spare no efforts to get it back now. I shall be terribly handicapped if I can't remember the moves."

While he was talking I suddenly noticed a small ladder at the top of Poodle's stocking, and just as I saw it there came to me one of those flashes of thought which are half memory and half instinct, and I remembered the sight of Doctor Schmutzig's fishing rod and the trailing hook which had followed him as he rushed away. And all at once I saw the whole ingenious plan. He must have clung with one hand to the back of our taxi and made a cast with the other, so that this passed through the window without either of us noticing it and hooked the envelope with the plans out of Poodle's stocking.

It was only a theory, of course, but when I explained it to them Poodle and Sir Hugo began to feel a sort of envious admiration for the Doctor's cleverness.

"Talking of angling," Sir Hugo said, "I remember once fishing for tunny in the Black Sea. That's a wonderful sport." He looked out of the window again and I saw that as he spoke his face was lit by the recollection of distant pleasures. "It's the weakness of fishermen, I suppose, as well as of adolescents to boast," he said, "but I really did land a rather curious catch once." He spoke in a deprecating tone that showed his pride as clearly as it showed his modesty in the event. "Really, we had a tremendous struggle, the boatman and I, and until we actually got it on board we were certain it was a tunny. But it wasn't. It was the proprietress of the hotel I was staying in at Odessa."

"That's an extraordinary thing," Poodle said with an interest that sounded fairly genuine for someone who hardly knew a lobster from an electric eel.

"What happened?" I asked.

"Oh, we had to throw her back," Sir Hugo said.

27

He paused for a little while. "By the way, the supplementary details of this plan, what about them?"

"Well, what about them?" Poodle said.

"Did he get those, too, your ingenious thief?"

"No," Poodle said. "You have them."

"Me?" Sir Hugo said, obviously astonished. "Now I wonder what on earth I can have done with them." He began groping about in the drawers of his desk, from one of which a *brassière* fell out. He pushed it back again without a smile, and as he saw Poodle looking at him he shook his head. "It's like the conjuror's hat, this desk," he said. "You know what you put in it, at least you think you do, but you never know what's coming out of it."

He rang the bell for Miss Plimsoll, and when she came into the room he asked her where the sub-sections of the B.O. plan were.

"You're sitting on them," she said. "Don't you remember? You slipped them under your cushion when the Dutch military attaché was here."

"Aha, yes! Inquisitive little creature he was."

Sir Hugo put his hand down the back of his chair and pulled out a blue envelope. "That's it. Thank you, Miss Plimsoll."

"Thank *you*," she said as she went out.

"Now, without this," Sir Hugo said, poising the envelope between his nose and his thumb, "I really don't see how our fine feathered friend is going to benefit at all by the plan he's got hold of. It's an impossibility to see how it could be worked without these details. You might as well try to load a service rifle with bananas or *chipolata* sausages."

He stopped and looked at Poodle as he said this with a peculiar fixity that seemed to come into his eyes when something was said in passing that distracted his thoughts from their objective.

"That might be rather a joke, don't you think?" he said with a faint expression of cheerfulness that was the nearest I had seen him get to being really jovial. "If we could somehow arrange for our new two-pounder Pom-Pom to fire a string of sausages when the War Office make their test." He turned towards the door, which was opened again by Miss Plimsoll as he spoke. A girl came into the room, and when she saw us she hesitated.

"You're busy?" she said to Sir Hugo.

"Not particularly," he said, taking his feet off the desk.

The girl was tall and in a conventional way she was beautiful. But there was a look of intelligence and animation in her face, which is a rare thing in beautiful women. She was instinctively and immeasurably *chic*.

"This is my daughter Vanilla," Sir Hugo said. Miss Hugo had that same dignity and reserve as her father, and she now transferred some of her lipstick to his moustache. She was the type of woman that I knew Poodle most admired, and no one, in fact, but an anchorite could have felt merely lukewarm in her presence.

For some minutes she sat quietly in an armchair, while Poodle and Sir Hugo outlined a plan for getting on to the track of Doctor Schmutzig again. Though the B.O. plan might be useless without its details of procedure, there were obvious objections to letting every inquisitive agent of a foreign Power know just what pre-cautionary measures we were taking against invasion. And what was in its way still more im-portant was the solution of the chess problem that Sir Hugo had begun to work out on the margin of the plan. If not actually vital to England's defence it was at any rate vital to Sir Hugo's.

Presently the door opened again, and Miss Plimsoll brought in a thick-set, cheerful-looking man wearing a bowler hat and a raincoat. He had a pair of sharp eyes that darted at you from behind pince-nez, and a cataract of plump chins that slid away from his moustache into a collar with two stiff but dainty wings. When I saw him I was never more surprised in my life. He was Chief Inspector Cheese of the Special Branch of New Scotland Yard.

Chief Inspector Cheese.

From time to time the paths of duty that we both minced along had accidentally crossed. It was the duty of his department to care for the safety of film stars, or of foreign royalty and diplomats visiting England. And as the official hospitality shown towards these people was arranged by the department to which I belonged, the Inspector and I had occasionally come into contact.

He gave me a perky nod as he came in, and seeing Miss Hugo he took off his hat and made her a little bow. I had already heard from Poodle of several occasions when the Inspector had shown a sort of bravery and judgment that was surprising in anyone of so crumpet-like appearance.

"Good evenin', Sir 'ugo. I 'ope you'll excuse me," he said: "only I 'eard Captain Grummond was with you, so I took the liberty of chasin' after 'im 'ere."

"What is it?" Poodle said.

"Doctor Schmutzig, sir. I've 'ad a call from Sergeant Merrylegs. He's been tailing 'im since you left the Doctor at the Carlton. It seems like 'e's makin' for the East End somewhere, and Merrylegs would like us to go down there right away. If we're not quick 'e's afraid we may lose 'im again."

"Then we'd better go," Poodle said. He got up,

and Inspector Cheese saw the pale pink under-clothes beneath his dressing-gown.

"You wouldn't be goin' like that, sir, would you?" he said. "I'm afraid it might be sort of mis-understood." He looked doubtfully at Poodle, who hurried out of the room, stepping out of his chemise as he went through the door.

"Have you a car?" Sir Hugo said politely.

"No, sir," Inspector Cheese said.

"Nor have I," Sir Hugo said, and he took out a pack of patience cards from a drawer in his desk. He looked across at me as he shuffled them. "You haven't one, I suppose?"

"I have," Miss Hugo said. "Don't worry." She picked up her bag as she said this and went out of the room.

Her father dealt out the cards in front of him with an abstracted look. Inspector Cheese and I waited in silence for a few minutes until Poodle came back. He was now dressed like a man.

"Good-bye," he said to Sir Hugo.

"The three goes on the four," Sir Hugo said.

Poodle turned to me.

"Coming?" he said, and that was all. I was never more surprised in my life. There was no indication whether he expected me to refuse or accept this sudden, almost peremptory invita-tion. But he knew me well enough to rely on my curiosity if not on my courage to see him through whatever might be in store for us. I agreed, and we went downstairs with Inspector Cheese. At the edge of the pavement there was a big Mercédès car with Vanilla Hugo at the wheel of it.

"Coming?" Poodle said to her as we got in.

She said nothing, but nodded to him and forced in the gear, so that we shot away, and as the car roared up Whitehall we lay on the floor in a struggling mass with our legs waving above us.

CHAPTER III

LIMEHOUSE BLUES

To the prosaic mind of that phenomenon called the average Englishman there is always something inexplicably glamorous about the East. He seldom gets there and so until his dotage, which occurs usually during middle-age, he treasures an idealistic belief in something that bears no relation to the reality.

But the few whose fortunes may carry them to the China Seas or beyond are quickly disillusioned. The sights and smells of the Upper Yangtse are a good deal less pleasant than you might be led to expect by peering through Hollywood's heavily incarnadined pince-nez, or by buying joss-sticks in the Brompton Road. Nothing is more swift and sure than contact with the fatalism of Eastern peoples to produce an opposite reaction in the occidental mind. An agent of the B.A.T., whose spiritual and ancestral home is probably in Putney, looks with suspicion upon birds'-nest soup or eggs matured with all the care that should be lavished on a *cuvée* of Richebourg, 1921.

But in most people's imagination there still

exists a good deal of hazy, celestial romance. There is magic in the name of Limehouse as potent as any in Lourdes, and there is probably as much jiggery-pokery in one as in the other. I can speak of Limehouse from my own experience, though I know nothing of Lourdes beyond what I have been told. Acidity combined with a certain lack of faith have usually sent me to Baden-Baden.

As we drove through Pennyfields I began to feel a thrill unlike any I had experienced in the German spa, except and unintentionally in the vapour baths. Dusk had already filtered out of the sky and the night was beginning. Inscrutable yellow faces peered at us from out of the darkness, or the inhabitants going about their business showed us inscrutable black behinds.

Poodle guided Vanilla through a maze of dingy-looking side streets until we drew up in front of a house with a fish bar on one side and a convent on the other. In the bar, under glaring acetylene flares, the Mother Superior and some pale nuns were pecking at fried fish and chips wrapped in the *Daily Mirror*. I wondered, as I looked at them through the steamy window, whether this gave added savour to the meal. You might have thought that a sister worth her whimple would have preferred the taste of the

Tablet. Perhaps in the convent there was some poor fish who was reading that very article in the *Daily Mirror* which the Mother Superior was chewing next door. Providence can ignore the principles of the novel and the stage, and sometimes it does not hesitate to bring about coincidences in real life that are almost as staggering as any that Sax Rohmer could invent.

Poodle knocked on the door three times. Presently a small panel in the upper part of the door slid back, and a roving eye looked out upon us. Poodle spoke to the eye in Chinese and it answered him in the same language. There was a short sing-song argument, and during it Inspector Cheese and I whistled Turandot's aria in soft accompaniment. After a little while the eye seemed to be satisfied by Poodle's explanation and it quietly shut the panel. Then the door was unbolted and slowly opened to let us in. The man who was guarding it was a short, blunt-faced Chinaman dressed in a blue smock and close-fitting black trousers. There was a flat, tweed plate on his head, such as provincial golfers are unhappily prone to wear.

He opened the door cautiously and held it so that not more than one of us should go in at a time. Inside there was a passage lit by a small lamp. Near it were hanging two bats, but these gave no light at all except on the habits of their species, and in this respect they were really rather absorbing.

Poodle put his hand into the pocket of his coat, and I knew as I saw him do this that his fingers were gripping the butt of a Browning ·45. It gave me a rather badly needed feeling of confidence. There was nothing for me to grip except Inspector Cheese, and he was already gripping Vanilla. But I caught hold of the sleeve of his mackintosh and adhering to each other like this we stepped into the house. The Chinaman silently shut the door and then went ahead, making a sign for us to follow him. As we moved forward the Inspector tripped over a chop-stick which had been left lying on the floor, and the whole lot of us went down like skittles.

"Oh, my!" the Chinaman said. "You tlip up. Hopee you no makum damage honalable botty?"

He was very polite and solicitous, and helped us all to get up. We reassured him, and then got back into the clinch and set off again sideways down the passage; like the Chinaman ahead of us this was narrower at one end than at the other. We passed through to the back of the house and went down some stone steps into a low room. The atmosphere was stale and thick and as we came in, a few dopey-looking faces were turned towards us and a few dull eyes looked at us with expressions of mild curiosity. There was

A few dopey-looking faces.

a low running buzz of gibberish that was interrupted for a second by our entrance. It was all rather like a banquet at the Royal Academy.

Along one side of the room there were two rows of wooden bunks, one above the other, and in some of these men were lying on rough mattresses; they were either sprawling in oblivion or whispering and arguing with each other. Some of them were asleep, and most of these twitched or muttered in their dreams like brokers on Contango eve. In one of the bunks a negro was slyly cheating himself at Miss Millican which he played with a pack of torn and filthy cards. Nearby a myopic Chinaman was lying, and from a crumpled newspaper he was picking the winners with the aid of a magnifying glass. In the bunk underneath him a sailor was picking his nose with a match.

There were some rickety tables on the floor, and round them were sitting a collection of people who looked about as dreary and raffish as any that you could see in the pages of the *Sketch*. We were guided between the tables to one at the far end of the room where the Chinaman left us and went through a curtain of beads hanging in front of a door.

We heard him speaking to someone and a girl's voice answered. Like most Chinese conversations it sounded as if it were an argument; then there was a squeal from the girl and we heard a sharp slap. The Chinaman backed out through the curtains with a rather self-conscious grin and then went away, nursing the side of his face.

"Missy, she come light along," he said as he went by.

In a few minutes a Chinese girl came out from behind the curtains. She had a tray with some slender pipes on it which were decorated with tassels of red and green silk, and she gave one of the pipes to each of us. As she turned to go the Inspector stopped her.

" 'Alf a minute, miss," he said. "I'd like a pot of tea, if you don't mind, and some buttered scones."

Poodle apparently thought this was not a wise suggestion, knowing in all probability the sort of things from which a Chinese scone might be made. He signalled across the table.

"O.K. I've changed me mind," the Inspector said, nodding to the girl: "I think I'll wait till I get 'ome."

I picked up the pipe that had been given to me and looked at the bowl; it was carved in the shape of a *bodhisattva* and it bore an odd likeness to Mr. J. B. Priestley. In fact, the impression it gave me of the Bradford Dumas was so strong that while I looked at it my thoughts jumped from the reeking, dingy atmosphere of the place into the clear air of the Yorkshire dales. The broad vowels of the West Riding were mingled all of a sudden with the pidgin-English and the babble of foreign tongues that was going on all round me. Imagination is a miraculous faculty. It leaps across time and distance in the space of seconds. Joubert calls it the soul of the eye; an eye that never shuts. In the close squalid quarters of this den, which I think even Fagin would hardly have esteemed, my mind suddenly lifted itself out of its surroundings and soared to the downs above Ilkley, where I had once seen a briar blooming in the morning mist, and from it I had picked a rose which I pledged that same night for the embraces of a Sheffield barmaid.

Vanilla took her pipe up from the table. She looked at it for a moment, rather as you might look at the frozen Serpentine before breaking your way into it. Then she put the long cane stem between her teeth.

"Someone give me a light," she said.

"I should go steady if I were you," Poodle said. He glanced at her as if he were not sure whether to be cautious or encouraging or frankly to admire the calm way she took the initiative in experimenting with the thing.

"Chinese tobacco, probably. You never know."

"We soon will, though," the Inspector said. "Still, you can only die once."

42

He cackled, and then snapped back the catch of his lighter and held it to Vanilla's pipe. She smoked it in silence for a little while. We three sat and watched her, though I think none of us had any idea of what to expect. But actually there were no consequences at all, or at any rate none were visible, and I don't know whether we were relieved or disappointed. Still, it presently encouraged Inspector Cheese to take up his pipe and light it. He sat with his head on one side for some time, and occasionally gave a critical puff.

"S'not bad," he said after a while, and Poodle and I were tempted by his equivocal judgment of the stuff to try it for ourselves. We picked up the pipes that had been given to us and both lit them, feeling, at least for my part, slightly daring as we did so. No one can say that the Anglo-Saxon character is not intrepid in experiment and adventure, but it shows an unusual wariness in approaching foreign cookery or any kind of drink or tobacco that is not familiar to it. The Englishman encountering *bouillabaisse* for the first time is inhibited with feelings much the same as Captain Cook's when he first stepped on Queensland's shore. I began to draw at the pipe very cautiously.

My tongue responded almost at once to the taste of a tobacco that was faint but rather pungent, and which seemed to be subtly mixed with a flavour that was like sherbet and linoleum. It was certainly unlike anything else that I had ever smoked. It was not Latakia, and it was not shag, but it had some of the characteristics of both; it was neither Rhodesian nor Sumatran, and nor was it Russian or Turkish; nor Virginian, white Burley, Irish roll or Shiraz.

I looked at Inspector Cheese. He seemed to be as puzzled by it as I was. After a few minutes he put down his pipe and sat staring in front of him, with his tongue slightly protruding.

"Funny stuff, this," he said. "Reminds me of a trip we once went, the wife and me, round Beachy 'ead and back on *The Dolphin*."

He gave a little smile, not a very comfortable one, and wiped away a ring of sweat that had gathered on his forehead. The room seemed to have become more crowded than it was when we came in, and I was beginning to feel uncomfortably hot. Poodle sat at the table and smoked his pipe with an intense preoccupied look, as if he were not quite sure of his own reactions towards the experiment. Somehow this seemed stranger than it might have been because the cause and effect seemed to be quite unrelated. The sensation, except for the taste of the stuff which was not unpleasant, was one of smoking an ordinary pipe, but the results were very different. It was rather as if you were eating a piece of Dundee cake that

44

turned into haddock as soon as you got it into your mouth.

I looked over at Vanilla; she was sitting back in her chair with her eyes shut and the pipe still in her hand. It seemed to me that she had turned a little paler than before, and in the stale, suffocating warmth of the room this was not surprising.

As I looked at her I realised that the atmosphere was also beginning to affect me slightly. There was a singing in my ears. To begin with this was only a faint buzz; then presently it seemed to resolve itself into Verdi's *Addio del passato*. I don't think I had ever seriously doubted my ears until that moment. They are ears that I have always been fairly proud of, as much for their honesty as for their size, and when I looked round I was relieved to find that they weren't, after all, playing a trick on me. The song was coming from a lascar who was sitting at the next table. He wore a reefer jacket and a greasy shapeless cap, and his hair hung down on to his shoulders. He was rather drunk, and had screwed himself round in his chair so that his head was unpleasantly close to mine; and quite quietly but with an exquisite timbre he was breathing Violetta's song into my ear.

Its effect in the circumstances was quite incongruous. When I was at a more awkward and

impressionable age, my Granny had once taken
me to hear Destinn's *Traviata*. It was a toss up
between that or Lottie Collins at the Tivoli.
Granfer plumped for Lottie Collins and so did I.
But Granny was a rather managing person, in the
sense that she usually managed to get her own
way, so Lottie went by the board and Granfer
and I were dragged off, appropriately in a growler,
to the Opera House. But we got our own back
during a *piano* passage in the second act when
Granfer unscrewed a bottle of ginger beer that
went off like a steam whistle. I was never more
surprised in my life, and Granny was soused, but
that, I'm sorry to say, was nothing unusual for
her. Anyway, since that evening I had not been
so curiously touched by the great aria as I was
to hear it so surprisingly in these surroundings.
The sound of it swelled and diminished as the
man swayed slowly backwards and forwards in
his chair.

I put my hand up to my forehead and I found
that I was sweating considerably, and I realised
all at once that I was really not feeling very well.
The walls of the room seemed first of all to be
swinging away from me and then closing in
again. The Inspector was floating in front of my
eyes like a kidney, and Poodle and Vanilla seemed
to be shimmering at a great distance as though
they were creatures in a mirage. I could no longer

The man swayed slowly backwards and forwards in his chair.

focus either of them properly, but it looked to me as though one of them had become pale blue and the other pale green. I dare say this effect was an odd one merely because it was unfamiliar, but Poodle's taste which was always perfect governed his complexion so subtly that against Vanilla's greenish pallor his leaden face somehow reminded you of the tones in an Aubusson carpet.

The lascar was now roaring out Violetta's song at full pitch, and the room seemed to be swinging round faster and faster, and though my hands and body felt chilled the sweat was streaming off my face. Suddenly Poodle loomed up in front of me, and I had to grip on to the table to prevent myself sheering away. I saw him pointing across the room to the line of bunks by the wall.

"Look—look!" he said. His voice sounded curiously hoarse and far away.

I shook my head violently to try to clear it, and for a little while the dancing pattern of the room became still. Then I looked over to where Poodle was pointing, and in one of the lower bunks I saw Doctor Schmutzig. He was smoking a little pipe like the ones we had been given, but he looked quite imperturbable about it. Apparently he was either used to its effects or indifferent to them, and he lay curled on a ragged sort of mattress quietly reading *Die Klosett Welt*.

48

Poodle stood up when he saw him and jerked Inspector Cheese to his feet.

"Come on—quickly," he said.

I pulled myself up from the chair so that the lascar, still with *Traviata* on his lips, rolled underneath the table. I was feeling so unwell by this time that I could only have made the effort because some instinct of danger seemed to warn me that in the next few minutes things were going to move pretty fast.

"I'm with you," I said.

Poodle said, "No," and pushed me back into the chair. "You can't leave Vanilla," he said.

I fought for a minute or two with my senses which were drugged and conflicting, and then the inability to get up again decided for me that I should be chivalrous but resigned. I dimly watched Poodle and the Inspector crossing the room and when they had got almost within spitting distance of Schmutzig he looked up and saw them. For a few seconds there was a sort of panic in his face, and then he deliberately blew a cloud of smoke at them out of his pipe.

Poodle stopped, but the Inspector went forward, beating the air with his handkerchief to get rid of the fumes. But they poured out of the Doctor's pipe in a great cloud. A moment later a bottle shot up through the smoke from somewhere or other and smashed against the electric light. At the far end of the room there was a glimmer that came through the half-open door, but as the smoke rolled out from underneath the bunks in great clouds we were left choking in the darkness. There was suddenly a great deal of noise and the sound of struggling; then a girl screamed. A table went over with a crash, and someone fell. Vanilla clutched my arm and I tried to draw her near the door and away from the smoke, but as we moved along against the wall I felt her hand slip away from me and she gave a cry. I called out to her, but the only answer I got was the crack of a chair leg on my skull. Suddenly my arms were gripped violently from behind and my ears from each side; and then my ankles were caught from below and a large hand was clapped over my mouth. As hands go I had tasted worse, but this one was not too unpleasant, except that as the pressure of it went on I slowly went off, so that I could hardly struggle at all. Then my brain seemed to reel over, and in a few seconds I fell on to the floor more senseless than usual.

CHAPTER IV

FULL FATHOM FIVE

I SOMETIMES think the gift of a coma, or of that Napoleonic faculty of self-induced and momentary sleep, would be more than a godsend. At company meetings, for instance, or at folk-dance festivals or at almost any moment of *Götterdammerung*, think what a pleasure it would be to drop off for a few minutes. But the more enviable of human qualities, like the ability to size up a man on sight, or a horse, or a bank manager, are things that are usually inherent and cannot be cultivated.

But perhaps, on the whole, it is better to sleep soundly in your own bed, if there is no other, than to toss about uneasily in the stalls of a theatre or at the board-room table.

Natural sleep, they say, is better for you, and if so less enjoyable, of course, than the usual forms of narcosis. The pleasures of whisky or hashish are definite, even though they may be dearly bought. But sleep seems to leave you with nothing but feelings of having wasted a certain amount of time in meaningless insensibility. To make it a really enjoyable pastime we should all take a lesson from De Quincey.

When presently I opened my eyes I was not conscious of feeling anything that I could attribute to a special cause. In fact, I was hardly conscious at all. I looked round me, but the only thing I was really aware of was a pain somewhere in my head that I was not properly able to locate. My body felt stiff and uncomfortable, and there was some kind of fur on my tongue which I thought was probably skunk.

I caught sight of some dials and levers in front of me which rather gave the impression of being in an aeroplane, or even possibly a railway engine, so I shut my eyes again and tried to think back on what had happened.

I wanted to know first of all who I was, and then where. There was also the question of why, but that I was prepared to leave to my parents. In my mind I ran through a number of people that I might conceivably be. I thought first of Professor Haldane, and then of Louis Bromfield, and then Joe E. Brown and Commandant Mary Allen. But I was relieved to find that none of these seemed to fit the details of personality that were slowly coming back to me, in a rather woolly and hesitating manner like lost sheep.

The last things I could clearly remember were Vanilla crying out to me as she slipped away in the darkness, and the knock-out crack which had

I looked round me.

been given me by some anonymous donor. But I could find nothing to explain how or why I came to be in the place I was now in. I opened my eyes once more, this time rather cautiously, since the light, though it was fairly dim seemed to set off a bunch of tiny jack-rabbit squibs just below the surface of my skull. I looked at the dials and levers again, but there was not one as far as I could see that was at all familiar.

From somewhere near by there was a faint throbbing, and there was a vibration, too, like that of a ship. And as I thought of this it somehow dawned on me that it was a ship; in fact, that I was on board a submarine.

I was never more surprised in my life, and I shut my eyes again quickly, feeling unequal to argument, even with myself; and as my first inclination was to doubt what I suspected, I wanted to avoid a quarrel by not looking round. Then I heard a movement somewhere behind me and a quiet voice spoke:

"Feeling better, dear?"

I turned my head rather incautiously with a jerk, and immediately a small buzz-saw was set off in the region of my brain. A large man with a rough beard and dressed in seafaring clothes was standing in front of some sort of control panel. He spoke without looking towards me, but kept his eyes fixed on a periscopic lens that was projecting through the roof; he was so tall that this came close down on to his head.

I asked him where I was. For some moments he peered into the periscope without answering. Then he clicked his tongue reprovingly.

"These fish!" he said. "Really! The things you see them up to in this what-you-may-call-it." He bridled as he said this, with a horrible lower middle-class prurience.

I asked him again where I was. Then for the first time he looked at me, and seemed to be considering whether or not he should give this information away.

"Well," he said slowly, "if you want to know, you're on board the *Nancy Brigg*."

"That's a funny name, isn't it," I said, "for a submarine?"

"Not when you get to know the crew," he said.

As he spoke a bell rang somewhere on the control board.

"Ah! Dinner's ready!" He said this with so much satisfaction that I thought he might have been starving for a month. "Come along, dear."

He helped me up from the floor, and for a few seconds my knees seemed to be loose in their sockets and my head spun round. I waited until things had steadied themselves a bit, and then he shepherded me through the doorway and into a passage. There was very little space anywhere

55

and a great deal of machinery on both sides. In their neat but intricate arrangement the submarine's intestines rather reminded me of the human interior, and there was even a pleasant, laxative smell of diesel oil. I felt like a piece of pudding passing through someone's digestive tract. I felt like a piece of pudding anyway.

We went through the submarine and came out at last into a small cabin; and there I suddenly saw Vanilla and Poodle and Inspector Cheese. They were sitting at a table with a meal in front of them, and at the end of the table between Poodle and Vanilla was Doctor Schmutzig.

As I came in Poodle saw me and jumped up. I was really so glad to see them again that for a few minutes our being in captivity didn't seem to matter very much. Sometimes between English people, even if they lack proper introductions, the presence of something unknown or dangerous brings out a sort of impulsive, mutual sympathy. Except for my friendship with Poodle we were none of us known to each other, at least not at all intimately, but at the same time I think we all felt rather relieved to find that no one seemed much the worse for anything that had happened since we parted.

Doctor Schmutzig, who was drinking soup and who had said nothing when I came in, now asked me to sit down and join them. Though his English

was bad he spoke it in a sort of fastidious, collo-
quial way, and he was certainly amiable enough
in his manner towards me.

He said politely, "You will sit with us, please?"

I said, "I don't see why not." And as there was
a fifth place I took it.

My friend with the beard had gone, but a
timid-looking man with a face like a chamois was
waiting on us. Schmutzig spoke to him in
German, and he gave me some wine, staring at
me with a rather coy look as he did so.

"Chateau Latour, 1924," Schmutzig said; and
he put his moustache back into the soup.

"Would it be indiscreet," I said, "to ask what
you intend doing with us?"

"Indiscreet? *Nein, nicht im geringsten,*" he said.
"But no good."

"We've tried all that," Poodle said. "He says
he doesn't know himself."

Doctor Schmutzig moved his head a little to
one side with the effect of a shrug, and in a
deprecatory way he said:

"For the time being you are in my hands all,
und sozusagen, I am in yours. What may happen
we cannot prevent, you or I, and we cannot
foretell."

"That's life," Inspector Cheese said, and he
gave his teeth a deafening suck.

Schmutzig said brightly, "It may be death

also." He held his glass towards Vanilla and said, "*Prost!*" Then he drank some wine.

This didn't seem to be a hopeful gambit for general conversation, and so nobody spoke for a few minutes. Then Vanilla, whose social conscience was more sensitive than any of ours and instantly reactive to dead silence, said:

"I hear they're doing Gluck's *Iphigenia* at Glyndebourne this year."

"You don't say!" Inspector Cheese said, probably no less surprised than the rest of us to hear this.

He and I then began to play noughts and crosses on the check table-cloth, marking the squares with our finger nails, and the others started talking of higher things. But presently Doctor Schmutzig got up from the table and said:

"You would like the freedom of the vessel—it is yours."

In the way he said this there was a sort of magnanimous irony that made me smile in spite of my feelings.

"I wish that I could make you better hospitality," he said, with his peculiar shrug. "But here, as you see, it is very much cramped."

We got up and went outside, but as Vanilla was going through the door he called her back; Poodle stepped into the room with her.

"*Fräulein* Hugo, please. *Einen Augenblick, bitte.* I would like to speak a minute with you."

58

"Well, you'll have to count me in, too," Poodle said. "What is it?"

Doctor Schmutzig looked at him and said quite suddenly, "Don't get tough."

He seemed for a second or two to become like some venomous bird. His eyes looked like a kestrel's, round and unblinking in their rage; and then as suddenly as this look had come into them it went out again and he was calm once more. He turned and said to Vanilla:

"I will not keep you long."

Poodle leaned up against the doorway and folded his arms.

"Anything you've got to say to her," he said, "you can just as well say to the rest of us."

"That's right. We're all friends 'ere," Inspector Cheese said.

He seemed to have a sort of optimism in the fundamental goodness of human relations that no evidence of corruption could destroy. Perhaps it was an illusionary faith, but it was one that had kept him and his sort going since the beginning of their existence. A life of perpetual mediocrity needs something more than hope to sustain it. Inspector Cheese was the emblem of a charitable belief in the world's good intentions and of the faith held by decent little men in the rectitude of each other's souls.

Vanilla looked at Poodle and then turned back

into the cabin. He tried to follow her, but she touched his arm and said, "No."

"No, what?" he said.

"No, thank you." She went inside the cabin and Doctor Schmutzig shut the door.

"Well?" I looked at Poodle. "Where do we go from here?"

"Let's take a look round," the Inspector said. "Come on."

Poodle said nothing. His foot was already on the rung of a short ladder that led into some place over our heads, and he swung himself up it. Inspector Cheese went up behind him whistling *The Roses of Picardy*. At the top of the ladder there was a space just large enough for your body to pass through into the room above. Poodle went up until his head and shoulders were on a level with the ceiling, and then he stopped short, so that there was a sudden impact between the seat of his trousers and the Inspector's bowler hat, which forced this down over his ears. Poodle looked about and went on up, and then the Inspector climbed through the hole after him and disappeared.

I followed them and was half-way up the ladder when something that may have been a premonition but was more probably cold curiosity stopped me. I listened, but there was no sound inside the cabin. I heard the footsteps of Poodle

A sudden impact.

and the Inspector on the metal floor above; they were going aft. And away behind me I could hear the gentle clicking and throbbing of the engines.

I stepped quietly down again into the passage, hoping to find some place where I could hide, with the vague idea of rushing into the cabin if necessary and saving Vanilla from a fate that is technically supposed to be worse than death. The situation already seemed so absurd and romantic that it was easy enough for me to dramatise it still further in my imagination. In point of fact, I had no doubt that Vanilla was quite capable of looking after herself, and in any case the cabin door was locked on the inside.

A sailor with a handsome but ladylike face came towards me. I stood back so that he could pass, and as he went by he gave me a shy smile.

"S'cuse me," he said, and wriggled his way quickly up the ladder, looking back at me with the eyes of a doe before he disappeared.

I walked slowly back towards the engine-room, examining the burnished neatness of the whole interior. Just ahead of me there was a short stair-way leading to a door that was half open, dividing the engine-room from the passage where I was standing. By kneeling on the steps I was able to look through the crack of the door without being seen. A sailor who seemed to be alone in charge of the engines was sitting not more than a few feet away from me. He was reading *The New Girl at St. Chad's.*

As I stood watching him my foot suddenly slipped on the metal steps, and though the noise of the engines made the sound almost inaudible he looked up and listened. I stood perfectly still and flattened myself against the lockers that were on either side of the passage. For a period of seconds that seemed like ages I had an uncomfortable feeling that he might be prompted to investigate, and if so the unexpected appearance of me crouching behind the door would probably have caused him to scream the place down. But as after a few moments nothing happened, I crept back down the passage and climbed the ladder to the platform overhead.

When I was half-way up I heard Vanilla's voice coming from the cabin. I stopped and listened. Doctor Schmutzig was talking, and then suddenly Vanilla screamed and there was a noise of struggling. Schmutzig shouted out something which it was probably just as well I didn't understand; and then all at once the door flew open so unexpectedly that I let go of the ladder and fell off it backwards, doing a perfect "jack-knife" on to the floor. I was never more surprised in my life.

Schmutzig was on the other side of the cabin.

His nose was bleeding splendidly and he was groping about on the little strip of carpet for his spectacles which had fallen near my feet.

"Are these what you're looking for?" I said as I lay on the floor, and I ground them into the carpet with my heel.

He looked up at me very surprised, and then he pulled the wine-bottle off the table and smashed it against the wall. The wine splashed out over the whole cabin so that you would have thought a bullock had been killed in the place; but the shattered end of the neck was left in Schmutzig's hand and made a very neat weapon to jab you with. He made a lunge at me across the table, but fortunately for me this was fixed against the wall, so that his range was short. Then he climbed up on to the table and made ready to drop on me, but Vanilla had somehow got up and out into the passage and she pulled me through the door by the collar of my coat. What my tailor would have had to say I don't know; but she got me out of the cabin, and kicked the door back and slipped its catch all in a second, so that Schmutzig was left inside.

I pushed her up the ladder in front of me, and we stopped at the top, listening in case the struggle had been heard by anyone. But there was no sound except the steady hum of the engines. Doctor Schmutzig, who had crashed on to the floor as the door slammed, seemed to have quietened down.

We crept along in the direction that Poodle and the Inspector had taken, and after poking into a number of places we peeped into the aft torpedo room, and there they were quietly waiting for us. Vanilla explained what had happened, and how, before my arrival, the Doctor had made a pass at her. Eventually she had kicked him on the nose with her heel and had got the key of the cabin from him. That was the point where I had dropped in. Up till then she seemed to have done her virtuous best to find out what he intended doing with us. But as neither of them were the sort to be easily compromised we were still in the dark. Though having made ourselves a fairly serious embarrassment to his plans, it was pretty clear that we were not going to be allowed to go at this stage of the game. We probably knew more already than was good for him, and besides, we might come in very handy in the form of hostages later on. The idea was not a particularly cheerful one, but as there seemed to be nothing we could do about it at the moment we settled down and made ourselves as comfortable as we could among the torpedoes.

"I tell you what," the Inspector said presently: "what we want is something we could threaten 'em with." He pulled a bunch of papers out of his pocket and began looking through them. "I've got a couple of blank summonses 'ere somewhere, if I can find 'em."

"That ought to put the fear of God in them," Poodle said rather brusquely.

"You may threaten its life with a railway share, you may charm it with smiles and soap——" Vanilla quoted, with a sort of quizzical irony in her voice. "Think again," she said.

We were all silent for a while. I looked about, but there seemed to be nothing that was handy for any sort of emergency. There was a rack over our heads, and on it were some drums of diesel oil which seemed as though they might have vague possibilities, if only we could think what these were. Then as I looked at them an idea struck me.

"I say, what about some boiling oil?" I said.

Inspector Cheese turned round to me with rather a tired smile.

"Don't be silly," he said. "What are we goin' to boil it in? My 'at?"

He sat with his feet tapping against a box like a coffin that was under one of the torpedo-tubes. Suddenly his heel caught against the lock of the box and the side of it dropped down, showing us a stack of rifles and ammunition inside.

"Well, you can take me for a nigger!" he said, with a look of complete amazement on his face.

66

At the foot of the box there was a service revolver but there were no cartridges for it; then the Inspector, after rummaging about, came on a small case with some orange sticks and a bunch of hair-curlers in it, and among these were about half a dozen slugs. He loaded the gun and handed it to Poodle.

Half-hidden underneath the rifles there was another box filled with some little frosted bulbs. The Inspector picked one out of the box and held it up.

"It's pretty, that, isn't it?" he said. "Do nice for the Christmas tree, eh?"

"It would do nicely for you, too, I should think," Poodle said quickly, taking it away from him. He pointed out a label on the box which read:

VICKERS-ARMSTRONG, LTD.
Ordnance Manufacturers to H.M. Forces

24
Chemical Tear Gas
Grenades

Vickers-Armstrong, Ltd., London, England.

"Well, fancy that!" Inspector Cheese said, "I'd put that back again, if I was you. You get larkin' about with one o' them things, you know—it'll only end in tears."

Poodle looked at the bomb, then instead of putting it back he handed it to me. I was never more surprised in my life. Then he took one of the rifles out of the box, and after he had loaded it he gave it to the Inspector.

"We're going to need your help, too," he said, turning to Vanilla. "Are you game?"

"Sure!" she said.

Inspector Cheese grinned at her, and said, "You're a brick, Miss 'ugo. You don't mind my sayin' so? I said to Captain Grummond, I said to 'im down in that doss 'ouse, 'That girl's got a face like a brick,' I said."

"That was sweet of you, Inspector," she said, with the sort of smile which if she had turned it on to Poodle or me would have made either of us forget our better natures.

"Now," Poodle said, "look here: you two had better go forward and I'll go aft. Shove any of the crew that you see into their own quarters, and lock them in. Be sure of that. And if someone tries any funny business——"

"I know," Vanilla said, "give them the works."

"The complete works," Poodle smiled. "Inspector Cheese?"

68

He handed it to me.

"Sir?"

"I want you to get to the engine-room. Clear the main ballast tanks fore and aft, then open the vent valves and see if you can bring us up to the surface as quickly as you can."

"Is that all? Blimey, 'e thinks I'm the Wizard of Oz!" the Inspector said. He looked at us blankly but with a sort of grin. "Well, I suppose I'd better try me tricks out."

"And if anyone's in there who tries to stop you——"

"I know," the Inspector said, and he put up a fist like a Virginia ham. "Bust 'em on the snitch, eh?"

"Right."

"O.K." He shouldered his rifle smartly and marked time on my feet, then he turned about.

"Bye-bye."

He marched out, and as he went the barrel of his rifle hit the top of the doorway so that the butt shot up and caught him under the chin. His head went back and his feet shot away from under him, and he landed on the floor with a whack. But a minute or two later he was creeping out into the passage, this time on tip-toe with his gun held in front of him, and his finger on his lips.

Poodle turned round and shook my hand.

"Good-bye, old man," he said, "and good luck. Look after Miss Hugo."

"I think it's Vanilla by this time, isn't it?" she said.

"If you say so," he said. "Good-bye, Vanilla."

He went outside with the revolver in his hand. I looked at the bomb which I was still holding, and I asked her what happened if you chucked one at somebody.

"I really have no idea," she said.

"That's a pity," I said. "Nor have I."

CHAPTER V

MAN OVERBOARD!

We went forward as Poodle had told us to do. I
still had the gas bomb in my hand, and remem-
bering that the slightest fracture of it would
promptly reduce both of us to tears I carried it
fairly gingerly. The possibility of Vanilla's beauty
and composure being spoilt by tears was distressing enough. But the fact that I was just as likely
to burst out sobbing in front of her was equally
mortifying; and if the bomb had been a statuette
of the Han Dynasty I could not have carried it
with greater care, though perhaps if I had
dropped such a thing my tears would at least
have had some motive.

We went along slowly and cautiously, each of us
with a conspiratorial air that came as much from
a dramatic sensibility that we seemed both to
have in common as from our nervousness, which
we both tried not very effectively to hide. I
don't really know what either of us expected to
happen, but our imaginations were keyed up to
a pitch that allowed us to anticipate almost any
kind of adventure, preferably one with a kick in it.

Except for the pulse of the engines below us,

which was steady but hardly noticeable, there was nothing that seemed to bring any reality at all to the situation. We moved about in the silence and oppressive air of the place as though we were beings from some chimerical sphere in the imagination of H. G. Wells. Time, at least as far as I was concerned, had ceased to mean anything, and space, though we walked in Indian file, hardly existed at all. Vanilla had, too, a sort of forthright logical quality about her that reminded you now and again of Ann Veronica or Marjorie Pope; but it was an impression that was not with you for long, thank God, and any other resemblance to a Wellsian heroine was contradicted by her *chic*, to which Bergdorf Goodman, Maggy Rouff, and Cartier had each lent a hand.

As she and I stood there in the gloom and stillness, wondering what on earth would happen next and when it would take place, it seemed almost as if we were the two last bankrupts left on earth. Our only asset was hope, and the liabilities against us were unknown. We could still hear the distant, inexorable thud of the engines and they sounded like the tumbrils of destiny rolling through Carey Street for the last time. As I looked again at the bomb in my hand I realised that proceedings of the kind we were now involved in usually ended with a stink of some sort, and I wondered how long it would be before we could earn our discharge from captivity.

As we crept past the door of the gentlemen's cloak-room a rather petty officer opened it and stepped out into the passage in front of us. He was a small man with a self-important air and an eye that seemed to rove rather too freely. After glancing at me with some suspicion he looked Vanilla up and down and then saluted her.

"Well?" he said.

"Very well, thank you," she said. "How's yourself?"

He looked rather taken aback by this, but she gave him no time to answer. "I wonder if you can direct me to the Captain's cabin?" she said.

"Won't mine do instead?" he said, smiling at her insolently.

Instinctively I stepped to Vanilla's side, perhaps more with the intention of lending her moral support than with the idea of clocking him, though it would have been a pleasure to do either. But Vanilla was in the enviable position of always being mistress of herself. And besides this, I knew that whatever my own feelings were, if we were to make the getaway we had planned I had got to control my temper, even though this meant standing by while Vanilla was insulted by this undersized nautical cad.

She looked at him with the eye of a bison kept

in cold storage, and I almost felt sorry for him having to face that uncompromising stare of hers. Then he nodded his head contemptuously and turned away, as if to pretend that, after all, he was quite indifferent to the company of either of us.

"Well, if that's how you feel about it," he said, "I may as well tell you we've got strict orders against speaking to any of the skipper's little party. If he was to hear me gabbing like this to you two, I'd catch a packet, I can tell you."

It was like a prophecy or an invocation to hear him saying this, because as he spoke I had been looking round to see if there was any means for enticing him back into the "Gents." And then with that sudden, quixotic generosity, which only Fate and one's godparents seem to possess, the means was literally put into my hands as the petty little officer was speaking.

Now and again the submarine pitched gently; it did so at this moment. The movement was only a slight one, but to steady myself I put out my hand against a stack of what looked like blue sugar bags and seemed to be filled with cement. But on the outside was a label that described the contents as "Ship's Biscuits," and though I felt slightly dubious about this I also felt absurdly proud and patriotic about the Navy's teeth.

I tilted one of the bags slowly towards me and

75

found that it was almost too heavy to move. But with an effort that I could hardly have believed myself capable of I finally succeeded in lifting the bag off the top of the stack. The dead weight of it almost dragged my arms out of their sockets, and as I stood there supporting it with every ounce of my strength, I remembered, for no real reason that I could think of, that my father had once gained a record at the Braemar Games for tossing the caber $5\frac{3}{4}$ inches, the shortest distance it was ever known to have been tossed. Compared with the weight of my packet I imagined such a feat must have been child's play.

"Why?" Vanilla said suddenly to the unprepossessing little naval object.

"Why what?" he said.

"Why mustn't you talk to us?"

He pulled a face that was meant to be rude, but was actually rather an improvement on his own.

"Because; that's why," he said, forgetting simultaneously his manners and his syntax. "And I tell you, if I do I shall catch a packet."

"That," I said, "seems almost inevitable." And as he turned towards me, I heaved the packet up into the air and jerked it in his direction, so that it fell down on him like a load of bricks. There was not even time for him to dodge, and without a sound he crumpled up against the partition

76

"Why what?" he said.

and lay still. I was never more surprised in my life. The worst I had expected it to do was for it to have knocked him groggy.

Vanilla shuddered a little and looked at me with a startled face. She hadn't even seen that I was preparing to throw the thing at him, and the sight of the officer falling down beside her like a bull under the thrust of a pole-axe was an agreeable surprise. She stooped and picked up a small automatic pistol that had fallen from his pocket.

"This may be useful," she said, and she handed it to me.

We quickly dragged his insensible body back where he had come from.

"Oh—but just a minute," she said; and she took the bomb from my hand and carefully placed it so that as soon as he recovered consciousness it would be smashed to pieces by whatever movement he made. When this happened, of course, the cabin would be choked with fumes at once, and the little officer with tears.

"What a pity we can't stay," she said.

We shut the door and ran quietly towards the crew's quarters, guided in their direction by the sound of singing. As we came near we stopped and listened for a minute. Someone among them had a concertina, and as far as I could tell there must have been a dozen voices at least. There was not much variation between them, but one rather lower than the rest was a booming contralto. The song they sang seemed to weave about like smoke in the stuffy air, and the volume of it swelled up sometimes and then diminished until it almost died away to nothing. It was like the sort of song you hear sung by impoverished White Russians in a Montparnasse *bôite*, if you can imagine such a choir of exiled princes singing *Knees up, Mother Brown!*

We came within a few yards of the open cabin door, and then we stopped. At present we were hidden from the men inside by the formation of the roof. But to reach the cabin we should have to step out into the light, and it was just a toss up whether we should be able to get to the door before they had time to slam it on us.

I whispered to Vanilla, "We've got to make a dash for it."

She nodded, and we shot out from where we were hiding and bounded towards the door.

The choir were holding on like grim death to the last notes of *Nellie Gray*, and they were so intent on giving full expression to the pathos of it that we might easily have shambled up to the door in the ordinary way for all the notice that was taken of us. With their eyes closed and their heads held in rigid juxtaposition they brought the song to an end; the long-drawn final breath, laden with tobacco and peppermint, echoed softly round the cabin.

Sitting by the door was the bearded seaman whom I had seen first of all in the control room. As if he sensed our presence rather than heard us approaching, he opened one eye and turned his head slightly towards us. For a few seconds he looked at us in this way without saying anything, then he nudged the man on his left who, without opening his eyes, nudged back. A series of knowing nudges were exchanged between them before the bearded person managed to draw his friend's attention to us.

I then decided that this was the moment to take action, and feeling absurdly conscious of how near to melodrama the realities of life can sometimes be, I levelled my automatic aggressively at the lot of them. But the result of this was merely to intoxicate myself with an unusual feeling of omnipotence, and it certainly didn't seem to arouse any fear in the crew. Then, as if to make things seem still less credible, I found myself speaking instinctively in the idiom that such situations seem to call for; in a voice that I hardly recognised as belonging to myself I said loudly:

"Stick 'em up!"

The man with a beard opened his other eye and looked at us blankly.

"Stick what up?" he said.

One or two of them raised their hands slowly above their heads. The man with the concertina let his instrument slip on to his lap, and it gave a rude, windy note. I was never more surprised in my life. The bearded man turned to him with a reproving look.

"Really, Gerald——!" Then he saw the others with their hands raised. "Oh," he said, and with the gesture of an odalisque he put up his own.

By now they had all surrendered, and Vanilla, whose resourcefulness never seemed to fail, was quickly knotting their legs together with a piece of rope that she had found on the floor. When each of them was tied by his ankle to the man next to him, she invited all of them to lie side by side on the table, and it really was a tribute to her charm to see how quickly they obeyed her. Though I was as inquisitive as any of them to know what her plan was I said nothing, but merely helped on those who were not quite alert enough by jabbing them persuasively in the kidneys with my gun.

When they were all lying prone on the table, so that it looked as if we were stock-taking in a mortuary, Vanilla picked up the end of the rope she had used to tie their legs with and explained her next move.

"I take this rope in my hand," she said, "and I pass it through this ring—so." She climbed on to a form as she spoke, and slipped the rope through one of the hammock hooks in the ceiling; then she pulled hard on it, so that twelve legs were raised as one from the table; there was a certain amount of twitching and protest from their owners, but she took no notice of this.

"I now take the end of the rope," she said, "and fasten it—so." She pulled the rope till it was taut, and this time there was some active squealing. Then she made the end fast against the handle of a locker which was a few inches from the floor.

"Now," she said, "would any gentleman like to come up and examine this rope?"

Being the only one who was in a position to do so without permanent injury to myself I stepped forward. I didn't doubt her ability to tie up a man pretty firmly in any position she wanted him, but I was beginning rather to enjoy myself and to enter into the spirit of the thing.

"Now," she said, after I had looked at the knots, "I am going to ask this gentleman if he will kindly assist me in removing the table." And as she spoke she suddenly seized one of its legs, signalling to me to take the other, and between us we tipped it sideways so that under the combined weight of the crew it fell over and they were left dangling upside down like a bunch of kippers.

"*Would any gentleman like to come up and examine this rope?*"

"And that, gentlemen, concludes the entertainment," said she.

If there was any applause she didn't wait for it, and we streaked out of the cabin and raced back towards the control room. Poodle was already there with Inspector Cheese, and between them a discussion was going on about the way in which the vessel ought to be brought up to the surface. They had already tried everything they could think of, but neither of them had ever been on board a submarine before. And if with them, as with me, this had always been a childish aspiration, it now seemed to have been fulfilled beyond all our hopes, and the prospect of staying on board for the rest of our lives seemed to be becoming more and more likely.

Not only the control panel, but the whole room seemed to be filled with dials, gauges, switches and levers of all kinds, and Poodle and the Inspector were standing in front of them in complete ignorance of how to read or operate a single one.

"Well, what would you suggest?" Poodle said as soon as he saw us.

"Why not twiddle a few handles?" I said.

"Don't be funny," the Inspector said. "What d'you suppose we've been 'avin' a game at all this time?"

For my own satisfaction I turned one or two

handles and a switch, but without any noticeable effect.

"Well, perhaps we should all twiddle them at once," I suggested, and as there seemed to be nothing to lose by trying this method we all began to push and wind and press everything within reach. The various dials and meters on the board showed sudden and violent reactions, and in some cases initials and remarks were pointed to that showed actual resentment. Bulbs flashed, needles shivered and bells tingled all around us.

Then we stood back from the board for a few minutes, and watched the instruments gradually recover themselves. There were slight jumps and tickings, but apart from these and the sound of my own heart booming with expectancy there was silence for a little while. Then the room began to tilt slightly forward; it was not alarming at first, but it suddenly took a steep swoop, and a few seconds later there was a terrific jolting impact which threw us clean off our feet. I was never more surprised in my life. In front of us a gong rang and in illuminated letters on a glass panel we suddenly saw the word "BOTTOM."

Inspector Cheese recovered before any of the rest of us. He scrambled up and shook himself like a retriever coming out of the water; then he went over to the controls, muttering vindictively, and began to move them about again.

"I say," Poodle said, "I think we should go steady after that."

"Well, if we don't do something about it," the Inspector said, "we shan't go steady nor otherwise."

"Well, I'll leave it to you this time," Vanilla said, as much out of tact, I imagined, as from her honest belief in the Inspector's infallibility. "Too many cooks spoil the broth."

It was my feeling, too, that this particular *crème d'asperges* had already been slopped about rather too freely, and so I decided, too, to watch Poodle and the Inspector do their worst. And nor did we have long to wait before their manipulations began to have some effect.

First of all the word "BOTTOM," which had been glimmering at us reproachfully, disappeared. And then by degrees the room righted itself; faint agitations took place in one or two of the dials, and a lever moved mysteriously of its own accord. We waited once more in a state of tremulous excitement until the angle of the cabin shifted slightly, this time tilting us all backwards and sideways. Then suddenly the whole submarine shuddered, there was a dull, booming crack as if a cork were bursting from some gargantuan bottle, and the ship seemed to leap up out of the water like a porpoise. In front of us, in bright letters, and accompanied by a sound like a piercing penny-whistle there appeared the word "SURFACE."

We made a dash for the conning-tower at once, and a minute later we were standing on the metal plates of the deck with the sea lapping round us only a few feet away. The sight of daylight again and the smell of the keen, salt air was a sensation that made the relief of Lucknow seem like a charade. From the yellow sky that was streaked with pale fire we could see that it was evening. The sun had already gone below the horizon, and we looked anxiously along this for the sight of a ship, but there was not even the smoke of one to be seen, nor a single bird to tell us whereabouts we were.

Vanilla was the first one of us to look behind her.

"Good God!" she said, "look there!"

We turned round, and five hundred yards away we saw Brighton beach and the old familiar Metropole rearing its fussy, bourgeois front towards the sea. There were times late in my adolescence when this had been a happy sanctuary for me, but I don't think the sight of it had ever been more welcome than it was at this moment.

Suddenly, as we stood looking towards the shore, there was a deafening boom from somewhere close at hand; the whole ship rocked, and from the bow port torpedo tube Doctor Schmutzig was plunged into the water and sent shooting underneath the surface of the waves towards the beach. I was never more surprised in my life. For him, of course, there could have been no other way of escape but this. Of all the risks that faced him he had deliberately chosen the one that was the most dangerous because it was also the most spectacular. He had fired himself off as a human salvo.

A second or two after he had shot out of the tube he ploughed his way up the beach, demolishing a line of bathing tents which stood in his track. Then he dragged himself to his feet and skulked out of view on the crowded promenade.

CHAPTER VI

METAMORPHOSIS OF MISS PLIMSOLL

LIKE most Londoners, I have a strong affection for Brighton, and nothing could have given me more pleasure than suddenly and unexpectedly to find myself looking on to its cheerful, vulgar, seething front. Sitwell *minimus*, though not a Londoner, has made an interesting *exposé* of Brighton, reminding us in the face of all its superficial attractions that since the days of Charles the Second the marvels of its neighbourhood have been chiefly amatory or municipal.

And so, to a town which for the best part of two hundred years has endured the reputation of a fashionable watering-place, and which has witnessed the fabulous eccentricities of "Prinny," and can also point with pride to Sir Harry Preston as having been its fairy godfather and suzerain, the appearance of a submarine in its waters naturally does not offer much excitement. So it was not until some time after we had risen to the surface that we were able to attract the attention of a boatman, but when he saw us he put out in a leaky coracle and brought us all ashore.

As soon as we set foot on the beach Inspector Cheese said that seeing we were here it seemed a pity not to make a day or rather a night of it. What about a go on the pier? He beamed at us expectantly, but was doomed to disappointment, because Poodle firmly suggested that it was our business to get back to London as soon as possible.

"What on earth do you imagine the Foreign Office will think?" he said.

"Ah! That's what you never can tell," the Inspector said with a touch of cynicism that was unusual for him.

And so in just over an hour we were dropping Vanilla at the house in Eaton Square where she lived with her father and mother, who lived with a retired Army captain called Bowater. This was an arrangement that apparently relieved Sir Hugo of several responsibilities, and so it was one that he welcomed. Besides, he and Bowater had been at Eton together, where they were rivals for the chess championship. That in itself was something of a bond between them, and though they had not then actually been in the same house, through Lady Hugo's ingenuity they were now often under the same roof without knowing it.

I found all this out from Vanilla as we sat together in the *Brighton Belle*, which tore away from its namesake as if it were anxious to escape its surroundings as quickly as possible.

The boatman brought us ashore.

After we had left Vanilla on her own doorstep we made straight for Whitehall, and as we pulled up in front of the gloomy building, which so well reflected the cumbersome and formal influences that deadened the architecture of its era, Big Ben struck half-past nine.

"Must be fast," the Inspector said, pulling out his watch. "I only make it nine-twenty."

Sir Hugo was not in, so the porter said when we arrived; but would we care to wait? He had said that he would be back at ten o'clock as there was some late business to attend to.

"Ten o'clock?" the Inspector said. "But they don't shut till eleven. That means 'e won't be 'ere for a good hour and a 'alf."

"Never mind," Poodle said, "we'll wait."

We followed the porter to Sir Hugo's room.

The desk was still in the same state of confusion as when we had last seen it. A tray with a whisky decanter and a syphon had replaced the tea things, but the golf clubs were still there, and a set of poker dice. The confusion among Sir Hugo's papers seemed to have increased. The floor near his desk was littered with them, and as I filled my cigarette case from a box on the table I suddenly saw that every drawer in the desk was standing open.

"Hullo," I said, "just look at this."

Some of the drawers bore marks as though they

had been forced, and the things from inside them were scattered round on the floor. The Inspector went down on his knees.

"It's too late to pray now," Poodle said. "Whoever's been here must have got away by this time."

The Inspector carefully examined the drawers and the desk with a magnifying glass.

"Amateur," he said presently, almost with a snigger. "Could 'ave done the job better meself. Must 'ave bitten 'em open, I should say."

In a corner of the room by the window a huge pile of documents and maps had been thrown; most of them seemed to have been taken from the desk, and from where we were standing there was a trail of papers leading up to this heap. As I was looking at it a large chart of Basutoland shifted from its place on the top of the pile without apparently being touched. I was never more surprised in my life. Though I'm not much of a believer in supernatural things, I could not help wondering for the moment whether this might not be some sort of ghostly *caprice de nuit*, the high jinks of some will-o'-the-wisp of Whitehall, Lord Palmerston perhaps. Yet I found it difficult to believe that any spiritualistic force would bother to manifest itself without some sort of encouragement. The business efficiency methods by which most well-known ghosts seem to conduct their non-existence are quite enough grounds for my own suspicion of their *bonâ fides*. Their obedience and regularity in suiting a medium's engagements, their adherence to a strict weekly time-table, (bank holidays excepted), does not convince me that they have so far "passed over" as to be beyond all human aid.

Actually until this moment my connection with spirits had been limited to a suburban *séance*, where a lady medium, who at the same time was not quite a medium lady, had gone off into a fit, during which she was said by her husband, a Mr. Cattermole, to be under the guidance of a Red Indian called Wet Blanket. Messages of a surprising irrelevance issued from Mrs. Cattermole, with a twang more suggestive of Bedford Park than Arizona. These messages were mostly for her immediate friends with whom the Red Indian seemed to have got on to the most intimate terms. But my own suggestion that Wet Blanket might put us on to a good thing for the Newmarket Selling Plate was rather ambiguously answered, though, with a Red Indian's knowledge of horseflesh you might have expected to hear of something dependable.

This experience, as I say, led me to have a rather dubious view of spiritualism, though the mysterious movement of the map that I had just seen rather shook my sceptical feelings. I looked at the pile of papers again, and rubbed my eyes.

"Tired?" Inspector Cheese said.

At that moment the whole thing began to move once more, and this time Poodle saw it too.

"Look!" he called out.

As we stared at it Doctor Schmutzig's grey astrakhan muff slowly appeared, pushing its way up through the mass of papers; and attached to the muff unfortunately was the Doctor himself. He was holding in his hand the blue envelope which had inside it the supplementary details of the B.O. plan.

You might have thought that the sight of the Doctor would have prepared us for almost any shock. And in fact, what did happen next was probably the only thing that could have astonished us more. As he stood there, knee-deep among the papers, Miss Plimsoll's face suddenly came out with a look of appropriate relief from underneath a copy of *Time and Tide*. I was never more surprised in my life. But since we had last seen her, she had changed in an extraordinary way. Her hair, which had been pale gold, was now almost black, and she had arranged it low down on her neck. She was no longer in the simple clothes she had worn as Sir Hugo's secretary, but had on an evening dress of black satin, so that her figure which was a remarkably pretty one was shown off to everyone's advantage. There were

95

jewels on her ears and round her neck, and though she certainly looked beautiful now, there was still that trace of hardness in her expression that I had noticed when I saw her for the first time.

"Good evening," Doctor Schmutzig said, and somersaulted through the open window behind him.

Miss Plimsoll gave a scream of terror and stepped back to the desk, groping against it for support. The rest of us leapt to the window. What we expected to see I don't know; what we did see, in the shadows thrown across the well of the building, was the Doctor crouching on the shelf of a service lift that ran close beside the window of Sir Hugo's room down to the kitchens in the basement. Already the Doctor was some floors below us, and the lift's momentum seemed to be increasing as it got nearer the ground. We watched it for a few seconds, and then with crash of splintering wood and ironwork it hit the bottom of the shaft.

But a second before it reached the ground Doctor Schmutzig leapt off it on to the tarpaulin cover of a lorry standing in the yard below, and whether by design or coincidence, this drove off just as he landed on it, shooting so closely under an archway that his muff was almost swept off his head.

"Good evening," Doctor Schmutzig said.

Inspector Cheese swung himself out of the window and dropped on to the fire-escape a few feet below.

"I'll be back again sometime, but don't expect me till you see me!" he shouted, and he raced down the iron stairway in the darkness.

Poodle turned away from the window, and I saw a look of relief in Miss Plimsoll's eyes as she watched him.

"He's all right?" she said.

"Yes," Poodle said, and sat down in an arm-chair beside Sir Hugo's desk. He was silent for a little while, then he looked up again at Miss Plimsoll. "Well," he said, "I've got to hand it to you this time."

"Then you didn't recognise me?"

He shook his head. "No." I could see that in a way he was reluctant to smile at her, though he did so as if he couldn't help himself. Then he turned to me and said, "I suppose I'd better introduce you. This is the Baronesse de Saint Tropez."

I was never more surprised in my life, though I didn't know at first whether he was joking or not.

"All right," I said. "I'm General Booth."

"Well, it may be a surprise but I assure you it's true," he said. "Oh, we've met several times before, the Baronesse and I."

"In fact, Captain, rather more often than you think," she said.

"I well believe that," Poodle said. "The Baronesse usually travels incognito," he explained to me, "but Dorothy Plimsoll's a new one. I've known Mrs. Reggie Roughouse, and I knew the Contessa Stromboli; and don't I seem to remember a little episode as Sister Wadding of St. Thomas's?"

The Baronesse nodded with a smile.

"In fact, I don't think I should be wide of the mark," he said, "if I told you that this young woman, incredible as it may seem, is probably one of the most plausible agents that we've ever had to deal with in our department; not to mention one of the most good-looking."

"Speech!" the Baronesse said, clapping her hands gently.

"Look here," Poodle said, suddenly dropping his bantering tone, "I'm afraid things are likely to become rather unpleasant for you, Baronesse."

"Unless what?"

"Are you imagining that you are going to strike a bargain with me?" he said, getting up from the desk.

She shrugged her shoulders. "You know my methods, Watson," she said quietly.

"Listen, Baronesse," Poodle said: "I have a considerable respect for your ability and your reputation in the service you belong to. And I also still have a certain amount of old-world chivalry left in me. But I may as well tell you, here and now that I don't propose to let either of those things interfere with my getting back certain specifications that have been taken from this desk, and also seeing that whoever took them gets what they deserve."

"I'm not sure that I understand you," she said, and she winked broadly at me.

Poodle's expression was stolid and philistine enough as a rule, but quite pleasant. He looked at her now as she spoke, and all of a sudden a curious ruthlessness came into his face. You could see that he was absolutely determined, not only on getting back the plans he had set himself to find, but on getting the Doctor too.

"Some days ago," he said, "a particular document was stolen from me; possibly you may know who took it. I have a pretty good suspicion already. To-night," he said slowly, emphasising the words with his fist, "an envelope is missing from this desk. That envelope was in Doctor Schmutzig's hand when we came into this room."

"And you want me to get it back, naturally?" the Baronesse said. She paused. "Well, I dare say I might be able to help."

Poodle took out his cigarette case and said to her:

"How much do you want?" He looked at her as he spoke with a hard, blank expression on his face.

She went a little nearer to him and took one of his cigarettes. The look in her eyes was unmistakable and provocative; it made me feel rather uncomfortable to be in the room, but at the same time envious of him. She said nothing for a moment; he gave her a light and then she turned away.

"Money isn't everything," she said.

I looked at her in surprise. She was clearly the sort of character who was *au fond* calculating and mercenary.

"Well," I said, "you may not think so."

"You don't know," she said. "The best things in life are free."

She looked at Poodle again. There was another pause, and then he suddenly screwed his cigarette out into an ashtray and said brusquely:

"No. I'm damned if I'm going to lend myself to an arrangement like this."

I was never more surprised in my life.

"Lend yourself?" I said. "Don't be such a fool." I was exceedingly jealous of his opportunity, and also I suddenly felt blindly and rather smugly patriotic. I said to him, "Surely you put the price of your country's safety higher than considerations about this sort of thing, don't you?"

"What?" Poodle said.

"I said, surely you put your country's safety higher than considerations about this sort of thing, don't you?"

"Well," he said slowly, "I suppose it hasn't occurred to you that the Baronesse may be what is generally known as a decoy duck?"

Actually this hadn't occurred to me, but certainly now that he mentioned the fact she did look rather a duck, if of a slightly exotic breed.

"And that if she once gets her talons into us pretty well anything may happen?"

"I've never heard of a duck with talons before," I said.

"Well, what about the dodo? That's a sort of duck, isn't it?"

"Thank you for the comparison," the Baronesse said.

Poodle still seemed uncertain, though it was inconceivable to me that anyone should hesitate over such a choice.

"I can't think why you're hanging back," I said.

The Baronesse looked at me as if she were surprised to find that I was ready to support her arrangements. She said to Poodle:

"Does this leech stick with us all the time?"

Poodle told her that I certainly did, and that that was the only condition on which he was

"*I can't think why you're hanging back,*" I said.

prepared to do what she wanted. Finally he asked her with what I thought was peculiar optimism to give him her word of honour that she would stick by her promise to help him get back the papers that were missing.

"Honour?" I said. "Honour your grandmother!"

"Why?" Poodle said with that uncompromising literal twist that I sometimes found was rather an irritating trait. "It isn't 'honour your grandmother' at all. It's 'Honour thy father and thy mother.' Baronesse, aren't I right?"

The Baronesse picked up a sable coat as she went towards the door.

"I wouldn't know about such things," she said. "According to what my nurse always told me I was a child of the Sphinx."

CHAPTER VII

THE HOUSE IN HALF MOON STREET

WE drove in a taxi as far as Half Moon Street, and presently the Baronesse said:

"Tell him to stop, will you?"

I called out to the driver and the man pulled up so sharply in front of the house that we were all thrown together in the most agreeable relationship. The driver was a stout, cheerful man, and he grinned as I paid him.

"It's usually the lady who shouts 'Stop!' " he said.

The Baronesse took a key out of her bag and opened the front door. Poodle and I followed her into the house. She apologised to us for the fact that there was no light, but the switch, she said, was at the other end of the hall. In the darkness my hand suddenly brushed against something that felt like a dog. I patted it, hoping for the best, and wondering which end was the least likely to bite.

"Now then! Now then!" the Baronesse said. "No tricks."

I was never more surprised in my life, and I begged her pardon.

It seemed to me that in the dark the only difference between sable and sealyham was whether you paid five guineas to be barked at or were bitten for five hundred.

A second or two later she switched on the light, and led us upstairs into a room that was filled with more pickled pine and bastard baroque furniture than Syrie Maugham had ever dreamed about. There was a coloured lithograph by Marie Laurencin on the wall, and a blind man could have told you that it was of a pair of dumb, frail girls with eyes like Elvas plums. Standing on a glass-topped table against the wall there was an enormous bowl of red poinsettias and white geraniums and tiger lilies. There was the inevitable stool near the window with the illustrated weeklies on it, and there were piles of cushions everywhere which were cut from the gaudy threadbare copes of old Spanish prelates.

In front of the fireplace there was the skin of a gigantic bear whose stuffed face, gaping bluntly up from the floor, reminded me of Lord Rothermere.

The Baronesse gave both of us drinks.

"This wouldn't be drugged, by any chance?" I said as I took the glass she handed me.

She smiled and turned away.

"I don't think anything I could put in it would affect your senses," she said.

106

I don't know why, but it gave me a feeling of self-satisfaction that she should have spotted me as being a pretty hard-headed type. But just to show her, I drank it straight off. She said nothing, but looked at the glass and then filled it up again.

For the best part of an hour she made herself charming to both of us, and she was an excellent hostess. Once or twice she suggested that I might like to take a nap on the sofa in the next room, but I had never felt less tired.

"He doesn't want to sleep," Poodle said. "He's as wide awake as I am."

"Wider, I should think," the Baronesse said in a voice that I thought sounded rather curt.

From time to time she gave us another drink, and then after a while Poodle said diffidently that he was sorry but that he had to remind her of the promise she had given him.

"Why? We've got the whole night in front of us," she said. "What's the hurry?"

And she poured another whisky into my glass. We sat on talking for a bit. Presently she looked over at me, then she said, "You look as if you're all in. Why not try and get a bit of rest next door?"

She had been so persuasive that I really began to feel as though I was a bit tired after all.

"Do you know," I said, "I think I will."

Then I forgot about it for a little while, and by the time I had decided to go into the other room I was so sleepy that it really didn't seem worth the trouble of moving. I dimly heard Poodle saying to the Baronesse that he didn't want to press her. Then she went over to him and sat on the arm of his chair.

"But why not?" she said. "I should like it."

I grew more and more sleepy. Poodle didn't move; he said to her, "It's a pity, you seem to be trying to misunderstand me."

"Me?" she said, and she made a sort of peck at his ear, it was not a proper kiss. But he moved his head too quickly for her, and I laughed.

"You'll find him a bit tougher than he looks," I said.

She glanced at me over her shoulder, then she said, "Will you oblige me by going and putting your head in a bag?"

In a way, it seemed rather curious that she should have said this, because that was exactly what my head felt like at this moment, as though someone had gently pulled a moist, warm tea-cosy down over my ears.

"It is in a bag," I said solemnly. "In a warm bag."

"It'll be in a cold one to-morrow, I bet," she said.

It seemed to me that she had rather a fondness

for making cryptic remarks of this sort. I puzzled over it for a bit, and then I imagine I must have dropped off to sleep for a little while. But presently I heard a telephone ringing, and I came out of my doze with a start.

"Hullo?" I said.

I picked up the syphon, which I thought was the receiver, and squirted it down my ear. But after fumbling round for a bit I found the telephone, and I said "Hullo?" again. There was no answer for some moments, and then in the distance I heard an operator's voice.

Again I said, "Hullo?"

"Hullo?"

> *"Who's your lady friend?*
> *Who's the little girlie by——"*

The operator broke in just as I was beginning the song.

"It's your call," he said.

"All right, three diamonds."

There was quite an appreciable pause after this; then he said:

"You asked me to get you a number, didn't you?"

"Get me a number of what?" I said. I began to wake up properly now, and I shook my head to get the soda-water out of my ear.

"What number do you want?"

"Who? Me?"

"No," the operator said, "your grandmother."

"Oh, she's got one already," I said.

For the first time the man seemed to show some definite interest in the proceedings.

"Oh, has she? Well, what is it?"

"I can't remember," I said. "Her number was up some time ago."

"Well, you're through now," he said.

"You mean I'm fired?" He didn't answer. "Look here," I said, "you can't do this to me. After all I've been——"

Suddenly Vanilla's voice came through. I was never more surprised in my life.

"Is that you at last?" she said. "Oh, I've been such ages trying to get you!"

"But how did you know I was here?" I asked.

"They told me," she said.

"They? Who do you mean? Whereabouts are you?"

"I don't know. I tell you, I don't know!"

Her voice suddenly sounded as if she were frightened of something.

"You mean you're lost?"

"Not exactly," she said, "not lost."

"But gone before?"

"Oh, don't ask me anything, please," she said, "I don't know."

"You don't know?"

I was never more surprised in my life.

"Yes."

"Well, make up your mind," I said.

"I mean yes, I don't."

"Oh. Yes, you don't?"

"What you mean is, 'Oh, yes you do,' don't you?" Poodle said.

I brushed the sweat off my forehead with my sleeve, and said to him:

"You keep out of this."

"Why? What is it? A wrong number?" he said.

"No, it's Vanilla."

He leapt to my feet when I told him, and took the receiver out of my hand.

"Vanilla! Where are you?"

"I wouldn't ask that, if I were you," I said. He looked at me rather surprised. "Oh, I mean, she just doesn't know, that's all."

They spoke together for a few moments, and as he listened to her his face grew more anxious. Once or twice he shot out a laconic question; but the whole thing seemed to be rather unsatisfactory, and finally he banged down the receiver and turned towards the Baronesse. She looked at him in silence for a few seconds, and then said:

"Well, where was she?"

"She's with Schmutzig."

"I thought perhaps so," the Baronesse said. She turned away and put out her cigarette. "He works quickly as a rule."

"Where has he taken her to?" Poodle snapped this question out in a way that meant he was having difficulty, as I could see, in keeping his temper.

"I don't know exactly."

The Baronesse went towards the window and drew back the curtains.

"Good," I said. "It's getting a bit stuffy in here, isn't it?"

She pointed down into the street, and I looked out and saw a car standing in front of the house.

"That car will take you to find her," she said.

Poodle looked outside at the car, and then at her.

"My God, if this turns out to be one of Schmutzig's little tricks——" he said.

And I could tell that though the recovery of Sir Hugo's problem and the B.O. plan was what he was still set on, the thing uppermost in his mind was Vanilla's safety. I had been with him in a number of tight places, and had been tight with him in as many more, but I had not often seen his expression as grim as it was just at this moment.

He turned to me and said:

"Come on." There was an unpleasant sort of catch in his voice.

"Swallow," I said.

He did, and then without saying anything

He   113

more he picked up my hat and went quickly out of the room. I picked up his and stumbled after him down the dark staircase, the hat, which was several sizes too big for me, swinging round my ears like a lampshade.

The Baronesse stood at the top of the staircase and watched us go down. The light coming from the room behind her threw a long shadow on the wall beside us.

"*Auf wiedersehen*," she said.

CHAPTER VIII

THE MAN WITH THE TWISTED ?

As we came out on to the pavement a man came towards us from a doorway. He said nothing, but motioned to us to get into the car. He was a thin, rough-looking man with a scarf round his neck and a cap pulled down on one side to hide his face. He walked with a sort of furtive slouch, and he fitted so unbelievably well into the picture, which had all of a sudden become like something out of a Sidney Horler novel, that I felt on the verge of laughing as if I were really reading one.

We looked at him naturally with rather suspicious interest, and as he came into the circle of light thrown from above by a street lamp, I suddenly saw that he had a twisted ? I was never more surprised in my life. I don't think that I am usually more susceptible than other people to the sight of deformities, but just for a few seconds I was rather sickened by the appearance of this one. Though I actually know several people who make me feel just as bad when I look at them, not many have the sort of interest which this man's peculiarity gave him. It had the same impellent but disconcerting quality as Donald Duck, and to prevent myself from simply standing and staring at him I jumped into the car.

Poodle got in after me and the car started. The inside of it was in darkness and though there was a bulb in the roof we couldn't find the switch. There were blinds over the windows, which fitted closely into slots on each side, so that there was not a vestige of light anywhere. And after a short time our senses of direction seized up, the car having cornered so quickly and so often that we were both dizzy. The way that it was being handled suggested that we were either on the Dodge'em with a novice driver, or were out with someone who thought no more of a traffic signal than if it were a pedestrian's life.

Pretty soon neither of us had the slightest idea of our direction. At one time Poodle guessed that we were probably not far from Bloomsbury because there was a faintly repugnant smell of stale highbrows.

Presently we drove over what seemed to be a bridge, and later on over what was undoubtedly a cat. By now we seemed to have got away from the traffic and I imagined that we were in the outer suburbs. But driving through these in complete darkness was nothing new to me, as I should have rushed through them in any case with my eyes tightly shut.

I suppose that we must have been driven for

nearly an hour when the car swung off the road into a rough drive, and a minute later it pulled up.

The man with a twisted ? jerked the door open. In the moonlight we could see the wall of a house just in front of us. It was covered with creeper, and the car had stopped a few feet from the front door which had a sort of loggia leading up to it. The man indicated that he wanted us to get out, and he jerked his thumb towards the door.

Poodle went in front of me, and as I got out of the car I looked up at the house and missed the step and down I went smack on the gravel. The man with a twisted ? lugged me to my feet, then he jumped back into the car which shot down the drive and disappeared. We both turned round and looked after it as it went off into the darkness, but the number plate had been covered over and there was nothing to see but an old satin shoe that was dangling from the luggage grid at the back.

We looked up at the house. The windows were barred on the inside by shutters, and as the moon came out from behind a thin rack of clouds we could see by the state of the loggia that the place was pretty well deserted. Grass was growing up between the tiles of the floor, and on the front door was a great rusty knocker that had obviously been innocent of postmen for some time. It was

shaped like a gargoyle with a face so like General
Goering's that it needed a good deal of self-
restraint on my part not to step up and give it
a thundering good bang.

Poodle and I stared at each other.

"Little man, what now?" he said.

I looked at the bell, which said "Pull," and
gave it a tug; the handle came out of the wall.

"Ah," said Poodle, "practical jokers, I see."

"Let's go round to the back." I said.

We stepped on to the path which was thick
with weeds and walked round the side of the
house. In front of us there was a lawn and on the
far side of it a great cedar tree which threw a
shadow half-way across the ragged grass. There
were flower beds on one side of the lawn which
were all covered with overgrowth, and start-
ing up from them were great hollyhocks that
looked like turnip ghosts in the moonlight. There
was a bed running by the side of the house with
some tousled-looking wallflowers in it, such as
you might see, of course, in any country bed,
especially after a hunt ball.

Suddenly Poodle caught hold of me, and we
stopped dead. I looked towards the base of the
tree where he was pointing, but I could see
nothing in the shadow underneath it. Then, as
I stared into the darkness I heard something
moving about on the dry needles that were

"Little man, what now?"

scattered on the ground from the boughs up above.

I whispered to Poodle, "What is it, d'you think?"

He put his hands on his hips and looked at me patiently with his head on one side.

"Now, how on earth should I know?" he said.

"Well, I thought you might."

"I can't even see anything," he said. "How do you expect me——"

"All right," I said, "all right."

"Well, then."

We looked towards the tree again. The footsteps had stopped. But in a moment they began once more. Then, on the other side of the lawn a great, clumsy figure appeared.

"Wallace Beery," Poodle said.

Its head looked as if it were too small for its body and seemed to be sunk down into its shoulders; its arms were a tremendous length. But from where we were standing it was impossible to tell whether the thing was some sort of animal or some sort of man; it definitely did not seem to be some sort of woman.

It loped slowly along dragging its feet like a bank clerk after a Whitsun hike. Presently, as it came towards us we got back into the shadows of the house and stood there waiting, and when it passed within a few feet of us we saw its face. It looked as though it were neither a man nor an ape, but seemed to be some kind of atavistic creature with the qualities of both. Its eyes were close and small, and as it went along it peered about it with a sort of myopic stare. The hair on its pointed skull was long and dark, and it had hands several sizes larger than a man's.

It was quite decently dressed, and as it stumbled by we saw that it was carrying an attaché case and an umbrella. It was singing to itself, too, in a low cracked voice, and before it disappeared round a corner of the house we caught a few words of Maud Valerie White's *Until*.

Poodle whispered to me to come on and I followed him, both of us treading on the border of the flower bed to deaden our footsteps.

The house was built in an odd, rambling way, and at the back of it there were some old stables and what looked like the servants' quarters. Presently we found a window that was conveniently low and looked out on to a yard.

I gave him a back up on to the sill and he looked through the grimy window.

"It looks like a maid's room," Poodle said, "but it's empty."

"Hard luck," I said.

Without looking round he jumped straight down on top of me, and we rolled together into a bed that was filled with nettles.

"Sorry," he said, "I slipped; couldn't help it. It was my foot."

"My foot!" I said.

When we got up we went on round the house looking carefully at all the windows to see if there was one that we might be able to open from the outside. We saw one at last that had a broken pane, and Poodle climbed up to it using the ivy on the wall of the house to help him get to it. He had almost reached the window when the ivy above him began to give way.

I roared.

He was clinging on for all he was worth and was scrabbling against the brickwork trying to get some sort of foothold, but wherever he got a grip on the stuff it simply tore away from the wall. Eventually he disturbed some starlings in their nest, and they flew out twittering, as I was, with excitement. Some of their eggs fell on to the ground and some of them on to the side of my head. I tried to wipe the remains off with my handkerchief, but it was rather as if I had had my hair shampooed with an omelette. Even then I was still struck by how funny Poodle looked, and the more I laughed the more irritated he got.

In the end he somehow managed to get hold of the window sill, and then worked himself up, just as he had done in the Intelligence Service, until he got himself into a position that was fairly comfortable. But things happening the way they were it was inevitable that as soon as he stood up on the sill the stucco underneath it began to crack and bits of brick and cement rained down on to the path.

By this time I was convulsed.

He clutched hold of the wall and eventually managed to push up the sash of the window; then he put his legs over and dropped down into the room. At once there was a splintering crash inside the house and a sort of tearing noise, as though a lot of rubble and plaster had fallen somewhere. Then, in a sepulchral voice that sounded very far away he said:

"I've gone through the floor."

At that I simply lay on the ground, and when I got my breath back I asked him if he had hurt himself. He said that luckily he hadn't, and that he was going to find his way down to the front door and let me in. So I walked round to it and waited.

I looked at my watch; it was a quarter to three. Five minutes went by and nothing happened. I began to wonder what my next move ought to be. The place was extraordinarily still. I could hear nothing but the tiny rustle of insects and small nocturnal creatures. From somewhere far away a dog barked once or twice. Then there was silence again.

I sat down on the steps of the loggia, and then started up again as a large tawny owl flew out from among the trees and flapped away on leisurely wings that made no sound. I was never more surprised in my life. I wondered how much longer it would be before it got light. There are some things to which darkness acts as a friendly chaperon, things like the age of Mistinguette, or the later utterances of Mr. Lloyd George. But it is definitely not an encouragement to sitting by yourself and anticipating the unknown.

I went up to the front door and listened.

There was somebody moving about inside the house; they were coming towards the door. The tread didn't sound like Poodle's. It was like someone dragging their feet along in a clumsy way. And while I was waiting there that instinct came to me which tells you unquestionably in moments of suspense that something you either hope or fear is on the verge of being realised, just as you can tell before it actually touches your tongue that the oyster between your lips is past its prime. I knew that on the other side of the door was standing the thing that Poodle and I had seen crossing the lawn by the cedar tree.

A wavering light came through the fan at the top of the door. Slowly a chain was taken off and the bolts were shot back. The door was opened, and at once a torch was put up close to my face,

A large tawny owl flew out.

so that the thing holding it was invisible to me. But its great hand came out of the darkness and twitched at my sleeve. I was beckoned inside, and as soon as I stepped into the house the door was slammed behind me so that it echoed all round.

CHAPTER IX

THE THING

THE light went slowly up and down, as if the thing were carefully looking me over. I could hear the sound of its breathing which was quick and heavy.

"What name shall I say?"

It spoke in that dry, obsequious tone that a good many old family servants seem to adopt, not so much to impress you with their indifference to the whole race of guests as to show their consciousness of a general social decay.

You generally find that the emblem of servitude, whether it be a baize apron or a starched cap, is now worn by old retainers as a sign of mourning for the days when the true art of service lay in knowing your place and in keeping it; which simply meant preserving the snobbish hierarchy of the old-fashioned servants' hall.

The prim and unctuous way the thing asked me for my name embodied all that kind of tyrannical nonsense.

"I think Doctor Schmutzig expects me," I said.

"Will you please step this way."

It held the light to guide me, and I could see

that the place was thick with dust. The marks on the floor where its feet had already been showed that no one else had gone into this part of the house for a considerable time.

There were great hoary cobwebs as thick as wool in every corner, and there were mice and insects. At the angle of a staircase an old copy of the *New Statesman* was lying. It was heavy with dust, and a few innocent but enterprising mice had nibbled at some of the pages; then, apparently seeing what they had let themselves in for, they had scuttled away to warn the others.

Suddenly the thing switched on a light which dazzled me for a minute, and then I saw that we were in a stone passage with doors leading off it here and there. There was a yellow and greenish-looking Morris paper on the walls. In some places it had begun to peel off and there were some fine funguses growing out of it, as if the pattern had come to life, though Nature's designs looked rather brighter, I thought, and a little less self-conscious than Willie's. There were places on the ceiling where moisture had dripped through, and though it had seemed quite a warm night when I was sitting outside on the loggia, here in the passage the atmosphere was distinctly cold, just as if Nervo and Knox had interrupted a Eucharistic congress.

When we turned a corner the thing stopped. It

listened at a door for a few seconds, and then it knocked.

A woman's voice called out from inside:

"You can't come in!"

It was the Baronesse de Saint Tropez, and when I heard her voice I was never more surprised in my life. There was silence for a little while, and then she said:

"Who is it?"

"It's the gentleman, madam," the thing said.

"Well, he'll have to wait, that's all."

The thing turned to me; I was fidgeting with excitement.

"Can't you wait?" it said.

There seemed to be nothing else for it, so I said that I would. It made a small bow, and then for a little while it stood in obsequious silence with its huge hands folded in front of it. Presently I caught its eye, and we both looked hurriedly away, though I was strongly tempted to stare. Now that I had the chance of seeing it at close quarters there was really nothing very alarming about it except its size, and this was exaggerated by its odd proportions which gave you an impression of power that was rather overwhelming at first. It had thin coarse hair and its pre-adamite features were not attractive, but its expression was mild and perhaps even a little smug.

After a few minutes it gave a slight, genteel cough, as if it were embarrassed by the silence. And then with its heavy, rather self-conscious walk it went up to the door again and listened. There was another voice coming from the room besides the Baronesse's, but whose it was or what was being said I could not hear from where I was standing.

Presently the thing smiled slowly, showing teeth like a dog's, then it covered the lower part of its face with its hand and tittered. It dropped the mien of the old family retainer altogether, and in a minute or two it beckoned to me with its hairy finger.

I put my head close to the door and heard the Baronesse laughing; then I recognised the other voice; it was Doctor Schmutzig's. I heard him laugh, too, and then say to the Baronesse:

"*Noch ein Glas?*"

Presently he told her in English the one about the ship's officer and the vicar without a candle-stick, which the thing said was a new one to it, and it giggled so wildly that it made me laugh, too; and when the door was suddenly pulled open by the Doctor we both of us pitched into the room, screaming with laughter.

The Baronesse was drinking champagne on a sofa by the window, and in the middle of the room there was a table with a cloth on it. There were also the remains of what had presumably been their supper, and they seemed to have done themselves fairly well with a pot of caviare and a cold bird.

The Doctor was smoking a cigar and had a champagne bottle in his hand, which he had wrapped round with a napkin, and as the thing rolled about guffawing on the floor he landed out at it with the bottle and shouted:

"*Steh auf, du Schwein! Was fälls dir ein! Geh' sofort unter!*"

The thing got up and ran across the room. Then it suddenly lifted up a trap in the floor; underneath it there were some steps, and it went down these, quickly shutting the trap after it.

The Baronesse smiled at me and lifted up her glass.

"Have some champagne?" she said.

"Certainly, have a drop?" the Doctor said.

He poured some into a glass and handed it to me across the table. Then he turned on his heel and went dancing slowly away towards the Baronesse, waving the bottle gently and singing as he went:

> "*Champagne Charlie is my name,*
> *Good for anything you like, my boys,*
> *Champagne Charlie is my name!*"

The Baronesse put up her hand and interrupted him: "Hark!"

"The herald angels sing——" he said.

"No. Listen!"

We listened, but we heard nothing. Then the Doctor poured out some more wine for the Baronesse and began to sing again, still waltzing sedately round:

> *"Champagne Herald is my name,*
> *Good for anything you like, my boys,*
> *Hark at Charlie's angels sing!"*

And after that he flopped down in a chair beside the table.

"There it is again," the Baronesse said.

She sat up and listened. This time I heard quite plainly a sort of cry. It seemed to me as if it was coming from somewhere below. The Doctor heard it too, and listened for a minute. Then he got up and put the bottle on the table and went over to the trap-door where he knelt down and listened again. Presently he lifted up the trap, and I realised that the sound was Vanilla's voice. I was never more surprised in my life. She was calling out something, but her words were muffled so that I couldn't make out what she was trying to say.

"What are you doing to her?" I said. "Let me go down there at once."

I tried to push the Doctor away so that I could reach the ladder, but he pushed me back from

"*Champagne Herald is my name!*"

it, and I had to shove against him to stop him closing the trap on my foot. We slapped and jostled each other for a minute, like ladies at the summer sales.

Then the Baronesse got up from the sofa and while we were struggling she pushed between us and lifted up the trap.

"Passengers off the car first, please," she said. And eventually she managed to elbow both of us out of the light and got down the ladder herself.

Then all of a sudden the Doctor seemed to change his mind, and he allowed me to go down after her. He followed us, shutting the trap behind him.

The steps were pretty steep, and the drop from the room up above must have been fifteen feet or so. The place underneath, which was so dark that we could hardly see, was like a high dungeon with a stone floor and pillared arches that supported the ceiling.

When we got to the bottom of the ladder I could see that there was some sort of light just ahead of us, but it was hidden behind a pillar. On each side of the place there were vaults and passages all in pitch darkness. We went on a few yards and then came out into the light, and there was Vanilla in a chair up against the wall. She was tied into it with ropes, and the man with a twisted ? was standing beside her. A gag had been put across her face, and when you think of the number of women in public life who ought to be stuffed in the mouth but who are not, it seemed a pity that here was a girl who was modest and not over-talkative, and who had yet been prevented from saying what little she had to say.

She rolled her eyes towards me, which was the first sign of any advance that she had made, so I winked back at her.

Poodle was sitting in front of her with his back against a pillar. He was gagged, too, and he was scratched and dusty. They had strapped him into a heavy, curious-looking chair that was raised slightly off the ground, and there was a kind of metal cap suspended over his head from an arm that came up behind the chair. I suddenly saw what the thing was, and I was never more surprised in my life.

"But, good God!" I said. "It's an electric chair!"

"Right, first time," the Doctor said. "Have a cigar?" He handed me his cigarette case.

"Thank you, I don't smoke," I said.

Then he turned to Poodle and offered it to him instead, grinning ironically.

"And he doesn't either," I said.

"He doesn't smoke?"

"No."

"Ha, ha! But you wait!" the Doctor said, and

he laughed very unpleasantly, I thought, and the thing laughed, too.

I looked round the cellar and saw that the whole place seemed to have been fitted up as a laboratory of some sort. In the middle of the floor there was a great bench littered with chemical paraphernalia, and there was a big cardboard box on it with a label which said:

BOTTOMLEY'S CHEMICAL FUN

A Collection of
HARMLESS AND AMUSING EXPERIMENTS
THAT MAY BE SAFELY ENJOYED
BY YOUNG AND OLD ALIKE

An Everlasting Treat

The man with a twisted ? tapped me on the shoulder and jerked his head, meaning me to follow him. He led me over to a box bound with iron like a Spanish treasure chest. When he put up the lid I looked inside, and there lying with his eyes shut and his bowler hat resting on his feet was Inspector Cheese. I was never more surprised in my life. The way he was lying, with his hands folded on his chest, made him look like the effigy of a crusader, except for the pince-nez. I stooped down by the box, but he didn't seem to notice me.

"Cheese!" I said.

"Oh, no, he's not dead yet," the Doctor said.

And he actually was far from dead, and as soon as I called out his name he opened his eyes and lay there blinking up at the light, but otherwise looking his trusty and authoritative self. Then he saw me.

"'Ullo," he said. "Fancy seein' you 'ere. My word, the world's a small place, ain't it?"

He sat up in the box and began stretching.

"I've just been 'avin' a bit of a nap. 'Bout the only place I could find to lay me 'ead in this God-forsaken 'ole."

Then he looked round, and over my shoulder he caught sight of Vanilla and Poodle. His eyes opened very wide, and he got up out of his box and said slowly:

"'Ullo, what the Musso's goin' on 'ere?"

He stared at both of them for a second, then went straight over to Vanilla and began undoing the cords round her ankles. But the Doctor took hold of his arm.

"You had better leave her, my friend."

The Inspector looked at him, annoyed.

"Well, I'm blowed!" he said, and he pulled himself away. "Leggo me arm, will you?"

He stooped down again to undo Vanilla's feet, but the Doctor made a sign to the thing, and said sharply:

"*Abführen!*"

The thing went up to the Inspector and lifted him away from Vanilla, just as if he were picking up a ninepin.

The Inspector squealed out in a voice so surprised and angry that it was quite high-pitched.

"'Ere, that's enough, that's enough!"

He was put down on the other side of the room, and then the thing stood there, to stop him going back to Vanilla.

"Inspector," the Doctor said, "if you will take from me my advice, you will not interest yourself in matters that are not concerned to you."

"Well, what's the big idea?" the Inspector said. "Tyin' these two up like a couple o' Christmas turkeys, eh?"

All of a sudden he slipped past the thing, and before anyone could stop him he had got to Vanilla and taken the gag off her mouth.

"Oh, thank God!" she said.

"Oh, and where do I come in?" he said. "For two pins I'd put it back on again." He grinned broadly at her, and then turned round to the man with a twisted ? "And you? What are you doin' 'ere, eh?" The man didn't answer him. He twisted the ? a little further round and looked at him, very much embarrassed. "Oh, yes. I remember you, don't I? Wasn't there a paintin' took last year from Lord Aldwych's 'ouse? And wasn't you the figger in the paintin', portrait like."

The man twisted the ? again and shook his head.

"Never 'ad your photo painted? Not by Ginsberg?"

I sometimes flatter myself that I know a little about painting, and I was interested as well as surprised that the Inspector seemed to know something about it too.

"Who?" I said.

"Ginsberg. G-a-i-n-s-b-o-r-o-u-g-h." He looked at the thing. "And what about you?" he said.

"Inspector Cheese," the Doctor said harshly, "I think you do not understand, but I want to make myself plain."

"You do?" the Inspector said. "Well, somebody's 'ad a jolly good shot already."

He looked round at us, and we all laughed. It was a favourite chestnut of mine.

Then the Doctor said:

"There are certain particulars that I at last have got after many great difficulties. And before they are given in the hands of my *Oberaufseher* no one from here must go. I am sorry."

"Do you mean to say we're going to be kept here," I said, "until you've skipped out of the country?"

"I shall not skip," the Doctor said with dignity.

"Well, until you've got away with the plans and things that you've stolen?"

"For an Englishman you speak in very plain language," the Doctor said. "You are not, then, a diplomat?"

"God forbid," I said. "But if you're only keeping us prisoners here, why the electric chair?"

"For Captain Grummond is a difference. He knows already more. Your *Sprichwort*, what is that?—a little too much knowledge is danger. I cannot risk at all that Captain Grummond shall say anything. By electricity you can do very much. *Paralysieren*. Then a man does not afterwards talk ever again." He sounded quite amiable about it. "But you need not kill him."

"Well, I wish you'd 'ave a go at my wife's mother," Inspector Cheese said.

"Now we are going. How long you are here depends until I am safely from the country. Someone then will come."

He jerked his head towards the ladder, and the thing and the man with a twisted ? went up it and opened the trap. The man got through into the room above and the thing followed him. Then the Baronesse went up, and she disappeared, too. The Doctor put his hand in the pocket of his coat and we suddenly saw the shape of a revolver sticking out through his jacket. He pointed up to the top of the ladder and said:

"And what about you?"

"When I am there, and I let down again the trap-door it makes at once the current to the chair. You will see." He bowed to us. "*Adieu.*"

Then he walked backwards to the ladder, still keeping us covered with his hand in his pocket, and all of a sudden when he was near the bench he caught his heel in the wires of some apparatus, and down he went. The Inspector moved quicker than I had ever seen him move before. They were rolling over and over on the floor in a second, and the Inspector was landing out for all he was worth, which probably wasn't very much, but it was quite enough to split the Doctor's eye in the first fifteen seconds.

Vanilla was thrilled. She was still tied to the chair but she was bouncing up and down in it and shouting out directions to the Inspector.

"*And* again!" she yelled. "*And* again! Mix 'em, Cheesey boy!"

The Baronesse and the thing looked down through the trap, and as soon as they saw the fight and heard Vanilla shouting they both knelt down on the floor above and began shouting too. In a few moments we were all shouting and yelling, and the Inspector and the Doctor were making a great round of it.

"Where's that left? *Where* is it? . . . *And* again! . . . Watch his head, ref! . . . *And* again! . . . On the old place, Cheesey!"

When they rolled on to the wires trailing underneath the bench Vanilla screamed out: "Ropes!"

And because I was so excited that I didn't even try to interfere she yelled at me:

"What a ref! Break 'em up, ref! He's afraid! Go on, break 'em up!"

And the thing called out: "Who paid you, ref? Mix 'em, Doctor, mix 'em!"

"On the old place, Cheesey boy!"

"Take your time, Doctor. Don't rush him. Take your time!"

The Baronesse leaned right over the trap, nodding and saying to the thing, as if she knew all there was to be known about it:

"He's a good boy, that Inspector. He can take it. Mix 'em, Doctor!"

"Break!" the thing screamed.

For a little while they got rather stuck below the bench, and when they rolled out from underneath it and back on to the wires Vanilla yelled out:

"Ropes again! *Where's* that ref? Tell us when you wake up, ref? On the old place, Cheesey boy! Downstairs, Cheesey! Downstairs!"

In the middle of it all the Inspector suddenly jerked the revolver out of the Doctor's hand and I put my foot on it and then picked it up, and at that second the man with the twisted ? leant through the trap with a gong and banged it.

They both got up and went into their corners. The Inspector was considerably blown by this time and he sat down on Vanilla's lap.

The Doctor made straight for the ladder. In a second he was up at the top of it and had taken a sort of hand grenade out of his pocket. He held it up over his head.

"Do not anyone move!" he said.

He was panting and very dishevelled and bloody. I always thought he was bloody anyhow, but the Inspector had made him a lot worse.

"Anyone moves, and you are in *Stücken*, all of you in pieces! You all see this what I have? He's here in my hand a bomb, yes."

The Inspector got up from Vanilla's lap.

"'Ere, I say! Chuck it——"

The Doctor chucked it, and was blown clean through the trap with a great flash and a roar that knocked us all on to the ground and shook the whole cellar. At the same second there was a crack like the breech of a gun bursting. The explosion had fractured a huge pipe at the back of the cellar and a torrent of water came rolling out on to us, foaming and tossing all over everything. I picked up a knife just as it was swept off the bench, and I splashed through the water to Vanilla and cut away the cords that were binding her.

Inspector Cheese was trying to get Poodle out

of his straps, but the water was bowling him over every time he stood up. It was pouring out in such a flood that everything was swept out of its way. He shouted to me to get Vanilla on to the ladder, and I looked up and saw that there wasn't a ladder any longer; there were only a few bits of splintered wood hanging below the opening of the trap.

CHAPTER X

FLOOD RELIEF

I WAS never more surprised in my life, and it occurred to me that I had better point out to the others the fact that it had gone, which I did.

"Well, I don't know, I'm sure," the Inspector said, undoing the last of Poodle's straps. "Seems to me like one of those days when everything goes wrong."

"Well, we've got to get out of this somehow or other," Poodle said, looking no worse than usual after the ordeal he had been through. He sat down on the electric chair again with the water swirling round his legs.

"What was you thinkin' of, then? Tryin' out the old Canute dodge?" the Inspector said.

We all got up on the bench so that our feet would be out of the water. But they were not out of it for long, and at the end of half an hour we had to put our legs up. And in an hour the Inspector was fishing with a piece of fuse wire on the end of a ruler.

Poodle said to him: "You won't catch much without any bait."

"I've got some bait," he said. "I've been pickin' my teeth for I don't know 'ow long."

At the end of half an hour we had to put our legs up.

In another ten minutes the water was beginning to get near the top of the bench.

"Do you suppose," I said, "if seven maids with seven mops were to sweep——"

"Shut up!" Poodle said. "I'm thinking."

"What with?" the Inspector said, and he went off into a peal of laughter.

Poodle, meaning to enter into the spirit of the thing, I suppose, gave him a shove, and the Inspector toppled off the bench into the water. When he came up, as if things were not bad enough already, he shook himself like a dog, and we were all soaked. After that we all grew slightly more depressed as the minutes went by, though inevitably the Inspector tried to keep all of us as cheerful as he could.

Presently he put down his fishing-rod and pretended to be rowing. Even this wasn't particularly funny until he caught a crab and went over backwards into the water again. For the second time in ten minutes we were all soaked to the skin; but soon after we had pulled him up again he was straddling on the bench and calling it "a mettlesome nag." Then he began to sing:

> *"Ride a cock horse,*
> *To Banbury Cross,*
> *Gave Lord Godiva,*
> *'Is grounds for divorce."*

148

He sang a few more stanzas which got pro-gressively nearer the knuckle, and then we quietly tipped him back into the water. As he was coming up for the third time Poodle suddenly leant back against me as if he were fainting and whispered in a voice of excitement:

"I've got it! I've got it! We're saved!"

We all hooted with relief.

"Don't you see what happens when the water gets a little deeper?"

"Yes, we all drown," the Inspector said.

"No, we don't. As the water gets deeper this bench will rise with it, of course."

"And then we shall float up until we can reach the trap, you mean?" Vanilla said.

It seemed so simple that I was amazed none of us had thought of it before; which, of course, is often the way. In a world where you already expect everything to be complicated it is not the most difficult things that elude you but the simplest ones, because most people, like Henry James, are deeply suspicious of simplicity. What can be easier, for instance, than handling the complicated mechanism of a car? And what is there more difficult than getting out of its way?

We anxiously watched the water as it rose, and even more anxiously the bench, which stayed exactly where it was. And by the time it was two or three inches under the water we realised that it was clamped to the ground. We all looked at each other.

"Who can swim?" Poodle said.

He knew already that I was as little use in the water as a varsity crew out of it; and I knew, too, that he was no better. The Inspector didn't seem particularly hopeful either; he shook his head.

"Not me," he said; "not since I 'ad me operation. I should turn turtle."

"A trifling metamorphosis," Poodle said rather dryly, as if this failure of the Inspector to come up to scratch was really due to selfish reluctance and not from any chronic inability. The trouble was, of course, that we all had come to look on the Inspector as a sort of *deus ex machina* whose resourcefulness was without end; and now to be reminded that gods, like mortals, are sometimes taxed by common ills was a set-back to his process of deification. Foot hygiene was a thing that was probably unknown to Olympus, but even Dr. Scholl's therapeutic genius has not found a remedy for feet of clay. It was Inspector Cheese's Waterloo, and it was like the discovery on meeting the woman of your dreams that she wears a *toupet*. There is nothing to do but grin and bear it, though it is advisable, of course, not to let her see that you are amused.

After all, the Inspector had done pretty well up till now and it seemed rather ungrateful to resent the fact that he was constitutionally or at least anatomically non-amphibious.

"I used to be able to swim," Vanilla said, "after a style."

"How do you mean," I said, "after a style?"

"Well, after the style of the Pre-Raphael-ites. I did a lot of sploshing about, but I didn't seem to make much headway."

"Then you couldn't really support any of us for very long?" Poodle said.

"Well, I can't actually see what that's got to do with it. I have my allowance," she said, "but out of that I have to provide myself with——"

"I don't mean that; I mean——"

"What you mean is," the Inspector said, "'ow the 'ell are we goin' to get out of this 'ole?"

"Exactly."

As the water was now eighteen inches above the bench we were standing up, and we were immersed as far as our knees.

"Well, I'll tell you," he said. "Listen: you see this 'ere——"

He undid his waistcoat with a flourish, as if it were the beginning of some sort of trick; then he pulled up his shirt, and underneath it was a salmon-coloured body-belt, which he snapped proudly against his flesh. Then each of us snapped it, partly out of curiosity and partly for the fun of seeing him wince.

"When you've quite done," he said, "I'll be glad to 'ave what's left. Now, if I was to cut my Roussel up into strips, and then twist 'em all together we should 'ave enough elarstic for a catapult, wouldn't we, eh?"

"It would surely be much simpler," I said, "if we were to play conkers instead."

"No. Don't you see? A 'uman catapult, I mean. Look!"

He began to undress quickly but with perfect decency, keeping his bowler hat on as a sort of talisman against offending our proprieties; and while he balanced himself skilfully on a corner of the bench he took particular care that none of us should see any more of his forbidden flesh than his ankles and the back of his neck.

Presently, when he had prised himself out of his rubber belt and was reclothed, he turned round again. Then he took out his pen-knife and cut the belt into several strips which he wound together to make a sort of rope.

"Get the idea?" he said.

The possibility of the scheme began to dawn on the rest of us, and as the bench was now under about three feet of water we helped him to fasten one end of the rope as quickly as we could to an iron staple sticking out from the wall, and the other to a bar that was fixed into the brickwork as a support for some shelves. There was enough

He began to undress.

resilience in the twisted strands of the belt to need all our combined force in stretching it between the two points, but when this was done we had the mechanism of a catapult that was more powerful and dangerous than anything I had ever dreamed of as a sadistic little schoolboy.

It had taken us some time to fix the thing securely at both ends, and while we were doing it the water had risen just above our waists.

"Now," Poodle said: "what about it?"

"Well, what I thought was this," the Inspector said, "the lightest of us——"

"That's you," the three of us said, pointing at Vanilla.

"Well, the lightest of us sort o' sits in the sling, see?—and the rest of us pulls it back from be'ind, and then lets go. And the one in the sling goes straight up through the trap. It's easy."

"And do they stay in a sling for the rest of their lives?" Vanilla said.

"'Course they don't! Look, it's ever so comfy. You'd be surprised——"

Somehow, as the Inspector was talking his foot slipped underneath the water and he fell back heavily against the sling. There was a deep rubbery twang, and then the Inspector was not there. I was never more surprised in my life. We had not actually seen him go, and so we peered down into the water, thinking that perhaps he might have slipped backwards off the bench and gone under. But there was not a sign of him. The sling was vibrating with a hum like a ship's dynamo, and as we looked at it we gradually realised that it had been effective beyond all our hopes, even the Inspector's.

We looked up at the trap.

At the end of twenty minutes we were still looking up at it, a little more anxiously and a little more vigilantly, and our hopes were deepening with the flood.

In three-quarters of an hour our eyes were still on it, but from the eyes downwards we were under the water, though Poodle whose upper lip was longer and stiffer than mine or Vanilla's, still had a little to spare before the water went up his nose; but she and I had begun to splutter uncomfortably when Inspector Cheese's head suddenly came through the trap.

I let out a cheer and let in a quart without thinking, as he dropped a rope down from above. It fell into the water with a plop and Vanilla struck out across the cellar. Poodle followed her, and I floundered along behind them with a rather breathless but energetic breast stroke.

"Sorry I was so long away," the Inspector said. "I got properly dazed, though, with the way that contraption shot me off. Talk about the flyin' trapeze, eh? And I'm blowed if I could find a

piece of rope in the 'ole 'ouse when I got up 'ere.
I nearly went and took the chain off the thing-
ummybob; only they don't 'ave chains 'ere, they
'ave 'andles. Right round to the garridge I 'ad
to go to find this piece."

By this time he had hauled Vanilla up and
she had scrambled through the trap. Poodle went
next, and then the rope disappeared and I heard
them walking away.

I yelled out and swam slowly round, cursing
them with every breath I had to spare.

Presently the Inspector peered very slowly over
the edge. He winked and dropped the rope down
a foot or two. I put up my hand and made a
grab at it, and as soon as I did this he jerked the
rope back again. I could see that he was shaking
with laughter, though he was trying to hide it,
and finally he let the rope down so that I could
grip it properly, and then with gusty chuckles
he pulled me up. At the edge of the trap Poodle
and Vanilla were sitting on their heels, and as
soon as my head appeared they whooped with
laughter.

"Oo, my word!" the Inspector said. "I 'aven't
'ad a laugh like that since Grandma died." He
took his hat off and mopped his head. "I never
seen anything so funny, not in all my natural."

He laughed again, and that set the others off,
and the more they laughed the more I was

irritated by them, and the less easy it was for me to control my own laughter. Finally, with murder in my heart, I burst out into guffaws that I shall never forgive myself for uttering. I suppose laughter is all very well in its way, but it can sometimes be as difficult to suppress as hiccups or scandal, and is often an equally unreliable gauge of one's true feelings. Still, I could see that the episode had its funny side, and, in fact, if Poodle or the Inspector, or even Vanilla, had been the one to have been left in the water there would definitely have been something rather funny about it.

We sat down on the sofa and rang out our wet clothes as well as we could, and then the Inspector brought out a flask of whisky from his pocket.

"This ought to keep the chill out," he said. "I found it just now in the sideboard."

He unscrewed the cap and carefully wiped the top, then he took a good swig and handed the flask to Vanilla. We each had a few gulps and then we had a few more, and in a very short time the effects of the cold water began to wear off. When we felt that we had all made a good enough recovery we got up from the sofa and then sank gently down on to it again. We made the same attempt once or twice before we actually got to our feet, and then we veered round very quickly and went in a body towards the French windows. We were through them and lying on the grass border outside before we realised that we ought really to have opened them first.

We had a certain amount of difficulty once more in getting up, but when we had managed this which we did with a good deal of giggling and balancing against each other, we rolled slowly round the house towards the garage. Earlier on, the Inspector said, there had been a motor car of some sort there. When he came to search for the rope he had seen it with his own eyes.

It was there still; and looked as if it had been, except for an occasional outing with the Old Crocks, since about 1908.

Somehow or other Poodle got it going, and then with a jerk and a loud clatter it trundled away, leaving Inspector Cheese and I who were sitting in the back, still inside the garage. I was never more surprised in my life. The body seemed to have become disconnected in some mysterious way from the rest of the car. But they backed towards us, blowing out clouds of thick smoke, so that when they had fixed us on again after a lot of tinkering about and we were ready to start, our faces were all blacked up, and off we went, looking like a nigger minstrel quartette.

We drove down an avenue of trees and out into

The old man scratched his head.

a lane. The dawn must have broken an hour or so earlier and the morning was still and cool; a heavy dew lay on the grass and on the hedges where foxgloves and honeysuckle were growing, and the air was filled with their scents. If at that hour the song of the birds had yet begun, it was drowned by the noise we made as we rumbled smartly down the road in a cloud of smoke.

Presently we met an old labourer who was making practically no pretence of clearing the hedge as he was supposed to be doing, and Poodle called out to him:

"Whereabouts are we?"

The old man looked at us, and then he looked at the car and scratched his head with his sickle.

"Up the pole, I should say."

"I mean, where are we heading for?"

"The ditch!" the man shouted, a second too late to stop us careering into it.

We got out and pulled the old sewing machine back on to the road, while the man stood by with a piece of grass in his mouth, shaking his head.

"Going to the carnival?" he said.

"No, we're not," Poodle said to him angrily: "we're going to London." And we got back into the car and drove off.

"Well, you're going a long way about it," the old man shouted after us. "That's the wrong direction."

Poodle turned the car round and we went back again past the old man who said to us as we crawled by:

"If you stick on this road it'll bring you to Maidenhead."

"How long will it take?" I said.

"Well, 'alf an hour, if you're walkin'."

Poodle said to him, irritably, "Do we look as if we're walking?"

"No; but you look as if you soon will be."

The old man sat down in the ditch, and we heard him laughing away to himself until we were out of earshot.

"Well, if I'm not crackers!" the Inspector said all of a sudden. "Maiden'ead, that's it, of course, I knew the Doctor 'ad a 'ouse near there."

In about an hour and a half, having dropped Vanilla in Eaton Square, we had reached White-hall. It was now half-past seven. We sat down on the steps of the building and waited.

CHAPTER XI

RETURN TRIP TO MAIDENHEAD

Soon after nine o'clock Sir Hugo bicycled up and we went with him straight to his room.

"Well, I'm afraid you've all had a pretty rough time," he said after Poodle had told him everything we had been through.

"And nothing to show for it so far," Poodle said. "But I'm not giving up hope, all the same."

"You're going to continue the search?" Sir Hugo said.

Poodle nodded. "And I believe that before long we shall get the plan and the Doctor too," he said.

Sir Hugo wiped a small piece of marmalade off his moustache and laid it on the blotter.

"Well, take care, my boy, that he doesn't get you first."

"I'm not the one who matters," Poodle said quite simply.

"Well, perhaps you're right." Sir Hugo looked at him thoughtfully. Then he turned to me and the Inspector. "But isn't it about time that all of you had some sleep? I've no doubt you must be feeling pretty done up."

"Oh, not a bit of it," Poodle said, opening the door. "We're all quite all right, really. What time shall we come back?"

"Shall we say five-thirty?" Sir Hugo said.

"Right."

We were downstairs and out in the street almost before he had had time to realise it.

"Well, pleasant dreams," the Inspector said. "See you when they open."

And each of us went off on our own ways.

Personally, I was feeling a good deal too restless and excited to think of going home and sleeping, but after a shave and a bite to eat at the club I dropped in at the Empire where there was a film with Dolores del Rio in it, and I went off to sleep straight away.

At half-past five we were all back again in Sir Hugo's room. He was at his desk with a little chess-board in front of him when we came in, and he held up his hand for us to keep silence. We sat down and waited for some minutes. Occasionally he jotted a few notes on a piece of paper and moved one of the men. At last he looked up at us with his rather melancholy smile.

"I must apologise," he said. "My queen was in a very uncomfortable position with a bishop. I had to extricate her." He began putting the pieces back into the box. "Well, what's your next move to be?"

"I'm taking off again," Poodle said. He looked at Inspector Cheese. "You'll join me, Inspector, won't you?"

"Well, sir, thank you very much." He wiped his moustache with the back of his hand.

I said that, of course, I would go with him, too.

Sir Hugo was silent for a minute, and sat tapping the desk with a paper knife. Then he said quietly:

"Somehow or other, Grummond, this plan must be found. The supplementary details don't matter so much because we have a copy of those. But that's what I ought to have done, of course; I ought to have taken a copy of my gambits," he said, shaking his head. "I tell you, my plan will revolutionise the whole of chess."

"And will the B.O. plan revolutionise the whole of B.O.?" I asked.

"Shut up!" Sir Hugo said wearily.

"Ah, we shall find it," Inspector Cheese said. He was such a determined optimist that you could never feel there was not a grain of hope left as long as he was somewhere about.

"What do you suggest we should do?" Sir Hugo asked.

"Well, if we had a warrant we could search the 'ouse, of course."

"The 'ouse?" Sir Hugo said. "Where do you mean?"

"Doctor Schmutzig's. 'E's got a big place down by Maiden'ead. I dare say we could get a warrant all right. But we'd better 'ave one or two fellers round the 'ouse in plain clothes like, for safety. It's a funny place, and you never know, not after last time."

"Very well, then. I'll arrange everything," Sir Hugo said.

He rang the bell and in a few seconds an anæmic-looking girl came in, with a shorthand note-book and paper cuffs. Sir Hugo looked gravely at her, and then introduced her to us as his new secretary.

"Never mind," Poodle said.

"Will you get on to Bow Street, Miss—Miss Flanagan?" Sir Hugo said.

"It's not Flanagan," she said; "it's Allen."

"Well, Miss What-ever-your-name-is, and say I want them to issue a search warrant at once. What's the address?" he said, turning round to the Inspector.

"Borden Lodge, near Maidenhead."

"Borden Lodge?" I said. "You're sure you don't mean bed and brek?"

Not even Miss Allen smiled.

"Tell them Inspector Cheese will call round for the warrant later on," Sir Hugo said.

Miss Allen looked at him dumbly.

"Is that all?" she asked in her insipid voice.

165

"That's all, thank you."

"You did say Bow Street, didn't you?"

Sir Hugo nodded with a kind, wincing smile, but she still waited.

"What's the number?" she said, and ducked quickly to avoid the ashtray.

A minute afterwards she dodged in again to say that Vanilla was waiting to see Sir Hugo, and should she show her in? She hardly waited for an answer, but shot outside again, and in a moment Vanilla came in. Once more she was looking cool and *chic*, and I saw Poodle's face light up with pleasure when he caught sight of her. They shook hands.

"Well, I'm afraid it's hail and farewell this time," he said. "We're just off again."

"We?" she said.

"*Oui. Nous partons tout de suite.*"

"But you're not leaving me behind?"

"You mean you want to come with us again?" he asked.

"Wild horses wouldn't stop me."

"Don't you think you rather over-estimate your strength, dear?" her father said.

"Well, I'm going, anyway."

" 'Oorah!" the Inspector shouted. "That's the ticket." He picked up his hat, and we all three said "Good-bye" to Sir Hugo, who kissed Vanilla.

"You'll take care of her, won't you?"

She ducked quickly.

"You can trust her all right with me," the Inspector said, looking like a particularly stolid and impeccable sheep.

"Thank you, Cheese, I believe I can," Sir Hugo said to him with a perfectly straight face. "Well, good-bye and good luck to you all."

We went downstairs, and outside Vanilla's big black Mercédès was waiting for us. We drove to Bow Street, but before the Inspector could get his warrant there were some formalities to be gone through, and by the time we were ready to leave it was after seven o'clock.

In about an hour we had reached Borden Lodge, and we saw it now for the first time in daylight. It was a large Victorian house of an ugliness you would not have believed possible unless you had seen it. Even then the idea of it being an hallucination would have seemed more likely than that it really existed. But there it was, and as we drove past we saw it through the trees. It was standing back with becoming humility some way from the road, and it had a thin, smutty plantation of shrubs in front of it.

We left the car a little way down the road and walked up to the gates. In a small copse near by, and as noticeable as the Eiffel Tower, were hidden three or four unmistakable plain-clothes police-men. Inspector Cheese crossed over and spoke to them. Then he rejoined us, and we went up the drive, followed with elaborate stealth by this *posse*. There were still a few dim, red streaks in the sky, but it was now nearly dark and the evening was hot and windless.

The house still looked as empty and as much neglected as it had on the night we had arrived there with the man with the twisted ?. The Inspector led us round to the back, and we stood for some minutes underneath the big cedar tree on the lawn discussing what our plans should be. Poodle distributed the plain-clothes men at strategic points round the house, so that in the event of any trouble they would be quickly available.

The French windows on the ground floor were partly open, and while we were still standing under the tree someone inside the house drew the curtains. But a small gap was left between them, and a minute or two later when a light was turned on in the room it shot a thin, bright ray on to the path outside.

"Let's chance it," the Inspector said, and we went towards the house, walking silently across the grass. A yard or two away from the window we stopped and listened. The Baronesse was inside talking to Doctor Schmutzig. Poodle put his hand into his pocket and I heard the click of his revolver.

169

The Inspector adjusted his hat, then squared himself up and with a slight cough, stepped in through the windows. The Doctor and the Baronesse were together on a sofa, and as we peered into the room over the Inspector's shoulder the man with the twisted ? came in at the door. He was dressed very unsuitably as a man-servant, and was carrying a large tray with some drinks on it. When he caught sight of the Inspector he dropped this with a crash that was like the heavens falling, and disappeared instantly.

The Baronesse and the Doctor sprang away from each other.

"*Verflucht!*" the Doctor said savagely.

His hand shot to his pocket, but Poodle had already covered him.

"Stay where you are, both of you," he said sharply, "and I warn you, there's no use in trying to get out of the house because every door in the place is being watched."

Then he turned to me and told me to take away the Doctor's gun, and as I ran my hands over the Doctor's body to feel whereabouts he carried it he suddenly gave a screaming giggle.

"Oo! Don't tickle!" he said.

I found his revolver in a holster that was strapped under his arm, but as I was pulling it out a great hand suddenly flicked through the door like a lizard's tongue, and out went the light. I fired into the darkness, and almost at the same time Poodle fired too.

"Bang! Bang!" the Inspector shouted.

I leapt forward in the direction of the door, and as I did so someone else leapt from the opposite side of the room and we met in mid-air with a smack that seemed to break almost every rib in my body. I was never more surprised in my life. Then against the half-light between the curtains I saw the silhouette of a huge figure with a small pointed head. There was a piercing laugh that was like a death-rattle, and the thing burst against the windows and careered away into the garden.

I scrambled to my feet, feeling completely dazed and went towards the door again, but as I dashed across to it my foot caught in the flex of a lamp and I crashed over once more, bringing down the whole thing on top of my head.

Poodle was shouting out to me to get the Doctor, though, God knows, I was the one who should have been yelling for him. It sounded as if a terrific struggle were going on. Every time I got to my feet and tried to make for the door somebody seemed to be milling out and I went spinning on to the floor again. Suddenly the lights were turned on, Vanilla having managed to work her way round the room and find the switch.

Poodle and the Inspector were rolling over and

over on the ground, and they were going at it hammer and tongs. But as soon as each of them saw that the other was not Doctor Schmutzig they stopped. The Inspector gave Poodle one on the beezum for luck and then they broke away.

The room had been pretty well smashed up, but there was no time now to stop and put things straight. Poodle called to the plain-clothes man out in the garden, who poked his head in between the curtains and showed us a black eye.

"Did you happen to see either a lady or a gentleman pass out just now?" Poodle asked him.

"No," he said, "but I nearly passed out me-self. *Something* come out, but it wasn't a lady or a gentleman. It was too big. Caught me in the eye; still, I think it was an accident."

"But no lady or gentleman?" Poodle said.

"Definitely not."

"Then that means they're in the 'ouse some-where," the Inspector said.

I opened the door and looked out into the hall; it was in darkness. The Inspector got out his torch, and presently we found the lights. Then we began a systematic search of the whole house. But there was no sign of either the Doctor or the Baronesse, nor of anyone else. We decided to go over the place once more, and so Vanilla and I separated from the others, having agreed on

"I think it was an accident."

signals that we were to make if any of us should find something suspicious.

Presently, when she and I were standing together on a landing near the top of the house, a low whistle sounded.

I whispered to Vanilla, "What's that?"

"It's a low whistle," she said. "Listen."

I strained one of my ears, already having strained the other in the rough-house downstairs.

Presently it came again, a long, soft note and then a short one.

I looked down over the banisters. On the wall I saw the shadow of someone moving cautiously up the stairs. I pointed down towards it and Vanilla looked over to see who it was.

"Well, what about it?" she said. "It's Poodle."

And when he came up we motioned him to stop and listen. In a few minutes the whistle came again.

"That's Cheese," Poodle said. "He's calling us."

We went on up; the stairs grew narrower as we got nearer the top, and when we reached the last landing the Inspector was waiting for us, looking down through a trap-door that led on to the roof.

"They're up 'ere," he whispered, "both of 'em."

He hoisted us up through the trap and out on to the leads. It was not properly dark yet, but the moon was rising and the sky was dusted with stars that gave a pale glitter. They were as thick as daisies in a meadow, and as I climbed out on to the roof one of them shot across the sky, like Harry Richman making for a Press photographer.

We crept behind the Inspector towards a chimney-stack, and on the other side of it we could hear the Doctor explaining tactfully to the Baronesse the relationship between Venus and Mars.

Poodle nodded to me, and we stepped out, one on each side of the chimney with our guns in our hands.

"Don't move!" Poodle said.

The Baronesse turned round with a start; she seemed to sway for a second, then suddenly she lost her balance and toppled on to the sloping roof. The Inspector bounded forward to save her, but she rattled away across the slates and in a second she had disappeared over the gutter.

As she fell Poodle glanced away from the Doctor for a second, and the next moment he was on the parapet. Poodle fired, and he dropped out of sight. We leapt to the edge of the roof and looked down. The Doctor had landed in a tree and was swinging from branch to branch like a gibbon in the jungle. He got closer and closer to the ground as we watched him, and then when he reached the trunk we saw him slide down it and tear off round the side of the house. Poodle shouted to the plain-clothes men below, but there was no answer.

"Look over there!" Vanilla called out all of a sudden, and we peered across the parapet on the other side. Dimly we could see the Baronesse hanging by the collar of her sable coat from the weathercock on top of the stables, and just as we saw her the wind changed and swung her round close to a chimney. She reached out and gripped the pot as she swished by, and then the collar of her coat came off and she was left clinging to the stack. She dropped on to the roof and ran over to a hoist that stuck out from the hay-loft; then in a few seconds she had let herself down by the pulley and was haring off along the drive.

"Where the devil are you?" Poodle yelled to the plain-clothes man.

"Here, sir!" the man screamed, standing just behind us. "I came up to tell you, sir, there was a man with a twisted ? come out the back entrance, but he got away."

"I don't believe any of you could catch an elephant," Poodle said to him brusquely.

"What for?" the man asked.

The Inspector had already jumped back through the trap, and he helped us down on to the landing; then we raced down the stairs and out into the garden. As we ran from the house the Doctor shot past us in a car, thumbing his nose as he went by. We streaked after him, and out into the road. On the footpath in front of the gates a shrivelled old wreck of a woman was selling flowers. Vanilla cannoned into her, and the old creature tottered up against the fence.

"Buy some lucky 'eather, lady," she whined, but we had no time to waste and had to chance our luck.

Then as we ran towards the place where we had left the car I realised suddenly that the Baronesse had added yet another impersonation to her repertoire.

I turned round to look for the old woman, but she had gone.

CHAPTER XII

ALL'S WELL THAT ENDS SWELL

THE Doctor had a good start, but ahead of us we could see the reflection of his headlights on the road. When we raced into a dip we lost them, then caught sight of the beam again as he came up on the opposite side of the hill. Sometimes the light skimmed along on top of the hedges or was invisible for a moment, and then it reappeared where the hedge flattened out or the car shot across some piece of open common.

Vanilla drove the Mercédès as if she were on the Belfast circuit and out to break all records. The wind screamed in our ears, and so did the Inspector.

"Anybody scared?" Vanilla shouted.

Her words were left far behind as soon as she spoke them. We all roared out, "Yes!"

"So am I!" she yelled back.

The car rocked us about like babies in a tree-top as we bounded first to one side of the road and then to the other, and the tyres screeched in protest as we were slung round the narrow corners of the country lanes.

We began slowly to gain on the Doctor. Then,

as we were drawing near Maidenhead his car suddenly swerved and stopped dead across the middle of the road. He flung himself out of it, and we saw him running down a path that led to the river. Vanilla jammed on everything, but even before the car had stopped Poodle made a spectacular jump from the running-board and landed on his backside in the hedge.

"Clever Dick!" the Inspector shouted, and we got out and helped to pull him off the brambles.

The path which the Doctor had taken led to a boat-builder's yard, and we ran through an alley at the bottom of the path and came out on to the river bank. Sticking out from it there was a jetty lined with boats and along the path there were sheds and slipways. Some of these had yachts shored up in them, and in the darkness with the moonlight shining on them they looked like great inverted sharks, or other kinds of shady City men, and threw equally curious shadows on to the ground. Behind the huts there were great piles of planks and plywood.

"Well, 'ere's a fine place to go and hide yourself in," the Inspector said. "Talk about lookin' for a needle in a timber-stack."

He took out his torch and started stalking round the yard. We searched the place cautiously for about ten minutes without discovering any sign of the Doctor. Once, as I looked round the corner of a shed, I jumped like a mustang when a face suddenly came round from the other side and said, "Bogey, bogey!" which was Poodle's idea, but not mine, of being funny. Certainly I was never more surprised in my life.

Presently we heard Vanilla calling softly to us from the other side of the yard.

"And the voice of the turtle was 'eard in the land," the Inspector quoted, as we went across to where the sound came from.

We had tried most of the sheds, and they had all been locked, but she had found one that had been left open. The Inspector flashed his torch inside. There was a bench in it with a circular saw, and there were bunches of laths stacked by the wall. The floor was piled high with shavings. He walked forward slowly, throwing his light about the place. Poodle followed him, throwing his weight about, as usual.

"Just put the torch over here, will you?" he said. "Now over here—now try it over there."

"If you want the three-and-sixpenny's," the Inspector said, "they're up at the back."

I was standing a yard or two from the door when it suddenly slammed. We all jumped and the Inspector dropped the torch. I stepped back in the darkness and tugged at the handle. We were locked in.

"Quick! Someone give me a light!" the

"Bogey, bogey!"

Inspector said, and by what I thought was an odd coincidence, just as he spoke a blazing hurricane lamp crashed through the window of the shed from outside.

In a very few seconds the whole place was alight. Sparks of sawdust and shavings floated up with the heat and rained down on to us, and flames and smoke licked up the wall like spotted snakes. We were all scrabbling furiously round the door, as if we were trying to get on to an underground train in the rush hour, except that none of us forgot we were creatures who were fairly decently behaved in the ordinary way. But in a minute or two the heat round the door began to blister the paint off it, so we had to move back to the middle of the room.

The walls were already on fire, but the Inspector leapt up on to the bench with his bowler hat like a crown of flames, and kicked out the window frame, just as if he were a storm trooper kicking out at some old woman. Then he jumped on to the ground outside, and we lifted up Vanilla, who was partly fried but fairly all right otherwise, and handed her out to him through the window. Poodle and I then got up on to the bench and at the same moment we both sailed neatly through the blazing opening and made a beautifully synchronised landing on the sawdust outside. If only an agent for Bostock or Ringling could have seen us we should have been a star act of the "big top" overnight.

I don't suppose that we had actually been in the shed for more than five minutes, though it had seemed almost as long and as frightening as the prospect of having to read *Gone With The Wind*. But the woodstack beside us was already blazing, and the piles away behind the shed had caught too, and were sending up swirling showers of sparks that fell all round on the other timber.

We ran down towards the water and saw the Doctor on the jetty. He was fiddling about with the painter of a boat, but when he saw us coming he jumped into it and quickly started up the engine. It spluttered at first, and then caught on, and the boat moved off just as we got within a few yards of it. Poodle did a sprint to the end of the jetty and took a flying leap just as the Doctor opened the throttle, so that the boat suddenly shot forward and Poodle missed it by about a yard.

My God, how we laughed!

We hauled him in on the end of a boat-hook, and then we all got into a launch that was lying up against the landing-stage. Even from there we could feel the heat of the burning sheds. The fire was still crackling and roaring and the glare of it lit up the banks of the river for some way on each side. The smoke rolled down on to the jetty, and great sparks hissed all round us as they fell into the water. Vanilla undid the rope that held us, and with Poodle directing it the launch streaked away.

I don't know how we were to have known that it was anchored, too, but we found this out after about five yards when the boat suddenly bucked like a wild steer and the chain snapped. The Inspector and I went over backwards as one man, and by the time we came up again the launch looked as if it were already half a mile away. But Poodle turned it and came back for us, and when we were on board again we shot down the river after the Doctor, who by this time had got fairly far ahead. We were close enough, though, to feel the wash of his boat which was a light but powerful one, and it rocked us very uncomfortably for a bit, until the river widened and we gradually began to creep up on him.

Once or twice in the darkness we had a fairly close shave. We were going full out, and the moon, like Vanilla, was pretty but not very bright, so that it was sometimes difficult to make things out until we were fairly close up to them. Near Shepperton we shot within a few feet of an old buoy that was not properly lit up. And when we got near Richmond we just missed an old girl in a dinghy. She was lit up all right, and so were her friends, and someone aimed a quart bottle at us as we loomed up out of the darkness. I had just taken over the wheel from Poodle and we passed across their bows with hardly a yard to spare. I was never more surprised in my life.

By now I doubt whether the Doctor was much more than two or three hundred yards ahead of us, and as we came up towards Battersea a police launch hailed him. He was going a great deal too fast for his own safety or for anyone else's, but he ignored the signals from the police boat, and shot the bridge at about fifty knots. The police turned their boat straight away and came racing up behind us, and in a minute or two they were followed by a P.L.A. launch. Both their syrens began to scream and the police brought their searchlight on to the Doctor's tail. When we got to Blackfriars the fire-float shoved off and joined us, having heard that something amusing was coming by; and from there onwards the whole river was in a state of commotion. The fire-bells were ringing and the syrens whining all round us, and ships up and down the wharves began hooting and whistling as we tore past. Other people joined us in all kinds of boats, and more police launches with searchlights and syrens came out from the dockside stations as we went by.

There must have been, I should think, twenty or thirty of us chasing after the Doctor, when all of a sudden he cut out his engine and stopped practically dead in the middle of the river. And the whole lot of us shot straight past him, shouting and yelling, and with the bells clanging and the whistles and syrens shrieking. Then, all of a sudden, he put his boat about, and in less than half a minute he was careering back the opposite way.

We all tried to turn round at once, but there was a good deal of craft anchored in the river, and coming up just behind us was a long convoy of barges, which straight away got involved with all of us. This was the signal, of course, for a slanging match between the bargees and everyone else. We were all hopelessly jammed up, and began shouting at each other through megaphones, and no one could hear a word that anybody else said because of all the gongs and syrens and the general hullabaloo that was going on.

But presently the convoy got clear, and then after a good deal of buffeting about and cursing each other we all got round and everybody seemed to cheer up. Then the row started again, even louder than before, and off we went.

The Doctor had got a better start this time, and he was at least a quarter of a mile ahead of us, but we gained on him little by little, and when he was getting near Westminster Bridge again his boat suddenly slowed down. We saw him frenziedly trying to restart the engine but it was no good, and after a second or two he took off his coat and waistcoat and put his spectacles into their case, and then jumped overboard.

But before we had had time to come up level with the boat he had jumped back into it, and we saw him take some small thing from the pocket of his coat, and then he dived back into the water.

Presently he came up and struck out towards the landing-stage under the embankment, but as we got near him he dived again. The boats closed in round the spot and the police dipped their searchlights on to the water. But there was no sign of him. Suddenly Poodle stood up on the side of our boat and the next moment he had jumped in, too.

When he came up he called out to us and said, "It's lovely and warm. Why don't you come in?"

All the same, he looked slightly uncomfortable and in a few moments he went underneath again. Vanilla went rather pale, and when he had not reappeared after about fifteen seconds she wrenched off a life-belt which was on the roof of the cabin and slung it out into the river. Poodle just came up again at that moment and it caught him right on the forehead. This time he went down more quickly, and when we saw him sinking Vanilla and the Inspector and I all jumped in together.

Three or four policemen at once dived in off

their launch, and then some of the firemen and the P.L.A. officers, and eventually there were about a dozen of us all swimming round after each other.

The Inspector shouted out:

"What about a game o' polo, eh?" He seemed for the moment to forget the possible conse- quences of his operation, and managed to keep the right way up without any difficulty.

But the rest of us were too busy trying to locate Poodle and the Doctor to think of aquatics. In a few seconds the police found both of them, and lugged them out on to the landing-stage. The Doctor had simply been foxing apparently, but Poodle was still a bit groggy, though he insisted on helping to pull Vanilla out of the water, and then he gave the Doctor in charge.

The sergeant of the river police took out a pair of handcuffs. But the Doctor waved them away and told him they wouldn't be needed. Then, before anyone could stop him, he put a small phial up to his mouth and swallowed something from it. Poodle and the policeman leapt at him. The Doctor struggled with them, and then he fell. I knelt down and picked up the bottle which he had dropped. It was Maclean's Stomach Powder.

I showed it to Poodle.

"All right, then," he said to the Doctor, "you

can get up again. But I'm not taking any more
chances. Give me the bracelets, Sergeant."

But the man who had been holding them had
accidentally snapped them on his own wrists in
the struggle, and he was marched away looking
rather a fool to have them sawn off.

The Doctor got up off the ground, and I saw
that he was eating something now.

"What are you eating?" I said, but his mouth
was so full that he couldn't answer.

Poodle saw him eating, too, and in five seconds
the Doctor was flat on his back again, with the
Inspector sitting on his chest and two more
policemen on his legs, while Poodle and I tried to
force his mouth open.

"Give me that boat-hook," Poodle said to one
of the men, and then the Doctor gave in.

"*Ja, ja, ich geb's schon,*" he said, and spewed out
a very unpleasant-looking, half masticated piece
of paper. I unrolled it rather distastefully and
flattened it out on the ground.

It was the B.O. plan, and it was pretty well
chewed up. But there on the margin in Sir Hugo's
neat writing and still intact was the solution of
his problem.

A policeman helped the Doctor to get up, and
he looked at Poodle for a second with a sly, sour
expression, then he smiled a little, and shrugged
his shoulders.

"*Mein Freund*, I salute you," he said. And he blew a raspberry straight at him.

The policemen hurried the Doctor away up the steps of the embankment, and I heard them both laughing until they were out of sight.

Vanilla folded up the plan. She looked at Poodle very thankfully.

"Oh, I'm so glad to have got it back at last," she said. "It means so much to Father and to chess. And but for you I would never have found it."

"And but for it I would never have found you," Poodle said.

The Inspector winked at me, and we began to walk up the steps together.

"And but for you, and but for me, and but for all of us," he said.